"Want to play hookey?"

Dylan asked lightly.

With a laugh, Abby tossed back her head. "Hookey?"

"That's right. You look like someone who never played enough hookey."

"I was never in one school long enough to work up to it. Besides, it's going to rain. What kind of fun is it to play hookey in the rain?"

"Come upstairs, and I'll show you."

She laughed again, but her eyes widened when she saw he was serious. "Dylan, the kids'll be home in a couple of hours."

"You can pack a whole day into a couple of hours."

He scooped her up, and her heart pounded as he carried her toward the stairs. It was thrilling, illicit.

Abby buried her face against his throat and murmured, "No one's going to have any clean socks."

"And only you and I will know why."

Dear Reader,

We at Silhouette **Special Edition** are very pleased to bring you this complete collector's set of *THE O'HURLEYS!* by award-winning Nora Roberts.

Just as each O'Hurley family member is a unique individual—Abby, Maddy, Chantel and Trace—so, too, does each of these four enchanting volumes stand alone on its own merits. Together, however, they create a complex, compelling family portrait, now completed with the appearance of *Without a Trace* (Silhouette **Special Edition** #625).

You won't want to miss a single member—or a single moment—so look for all four volumes: *The Last Honest Woman*, *Dance to the Piper*, *Skin Deep* and now, *Without a Trace*. Meet *THE O'HURLEYS!*, united at last. We think you'll be glad you did.

Best wishes,

The Editors

NORA ROBERTS
The Last Honest Woman

Silhouette Special Edition

Published by Silhouette Books New York

America's Publisher of Contemporary Romance

For Terri, Kerri and Sherri,
who know what it's like to be one of three

SILHOUETTE BOOKS
300 East 42nd St., New York, N.Y. 10017

ISBN: 0-373-48231-0

First Silhouette Books printing May 1988
Second Silhouette Books printing October 1990

NORA ROBERTS

is one of Silhouette Books' most popular and prolific authors. She has written for the Silhouette Romance, Silhouette Special Edition and Silhouette Intimate Moments lines, as well as contributing stories to *Silhouette Christmas Stories 1986* and to the 1989 *Silhouette Summer Sizzler*.

When we published the four-book MacGregor Series, readers wrote in requesting the parents' story—and Nora Roberts responded by writing *For Now, Forever*. When we published the fifth MacGregor book, we reissued the first four. When Nora Roberts wrote THE O'HURLEYS! about triplet sisters, readers clamored for the story of their elusive older brother. Silhouette Books is pleased to present *Without a Trace*, along with reissuing *The Last Honest Woman*, *Dance to the Piper* and *Skin Deep*. When Silhouette asked Nora to comment on the miniseries, she said:

"Writing interlocking stories is always a pleasure. I get such a kick out of discovering what happened to the characters once their particular book closed! With the O'Hurleys, I discovered a family I could admire, a family I could laugh with and hurt for. I'm glad I had the chance to know them, and I hope that you'll feel the same way."

And for MacGregor fans, look for a collection of historical Christmas stories in November for a look at the early MacGregor clan.

THE O'HURLEYS!
Book One: Abby's Story

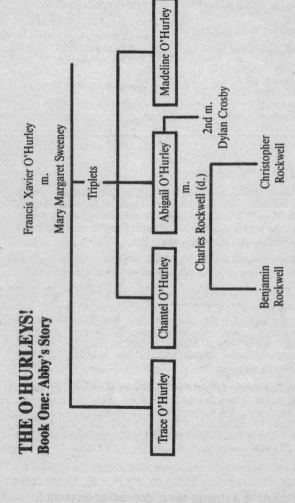

Francis Xavier O'Hurley
m.
Mary Margaret Sweeney

Triplets

Trace O'Hurley

Chantel O'Hurley

Abigail O'Hurley
m.
Charles Rockwell (d.)

2nd m.
Dylan Crosby

Benjamin Rockwell

Christopher Rockwell

Madeline O'Hurley

Prologue

Y‌ou can yell all you want, Mrs. O'Hurley.''

Her breath came in gasps. Sweat rolled down her temples as she dug her fingers into the side of the gurney and braced herself. "Molly O'Hurley doesn't yell her babies into the world.''

She wasn't a big woman, but her voice, even at a normal tone, reached all corners of the room. It had a lilting, musical sound, though she had to dig for the strength to use it. She'd been rushed into the hospital by her husband only minutes before in the last stages of labor.

There'd been no time to prep her, no time for comforting words or hand-holding. The obstetrician on call had taken one look and had her rolled into the delivery room fully dressed.

Most women would have been afraid, surrounded by strangers in a strange town, depending on them for her life and for the life of the baby that was fighting its way into the world. She was. But she'd be damned if she'd admit it.

"A tough one, are you?" The doctor signaled for a nurse to wipe his brow. The heating in the delivery room was working overtime.

"All the O'Hurleys are tough." She managed to say, but she wanted to yell. God, she wanted to as the pain screamed through her. The baby was coming early. She could only pray it wasn't too early. The contractions piled one on top of another, giving her no time to recharge for the next.

"We can be grateful your train wasn't five minutes later, or you'd be having this baby in the club car." She was fully dilated, and the baby was crowning. "Don't bear down yet, pant."

She cursed him with all the expertise she'd developed in seven years of living with her Francis and seven more of playing the clubs in every grimy town from L.A. to the Catskills. He only clucked his tongue at her as she breathed like a steam engine and glared.

"That's fine, that's fine now. And here we go. Push, Mrs. O'Hurley. Let's bring this baby out with a bang."

"I'll give you a bang," she promised, and pushed through the last dizzying pain. The baby came out with a wail that echoed off the walls of the delivery room. Molly watched, tears streaming as the doctor turned the small head, the shoulders, then the torso. "It's a girl." Laughing, she fell back. A girl. She'd done it. And wouldn't Francis be proud? Exhausted, Molly listened to her daughter's first cries of life.

"Didn't have to give this one a slap on the bottom," the doctor commented. Small, he thought, maybe five pounds tops. "She's no heavyweight, Mrs. O'Hurley, but she looks good as gold."

"Of course she is. Listen to those lungs. She'll knock them out of the back row. A few weeks ahead of schedule, but... Oh, sweet God."

As the new contraction hit, Molly pushed herself up.

"Hold her." The doctor passed the baby to a nurse and nodded to another to brace Molly's shoulders. "Looks like your daughter had company."

"Another?" Between pain and delirium, Molly started to laugh. There was nothing hysterical about it, but something robust and daring. "Damn you, Frank. You always manage to surprise me."

The man in the waiting room paced, but there was a spring to his step, even as he checked his watch for the fifth time in three minutes. He was a man who spent as much time dancing as walking. He was slim and spry, with a perpetual optimism gleaming in his eyes. Now and again he'd pass by the little boy half dozing in a chair and rub his hand over the top of his nodding head.

"A baby brother or sister for you, Trace. They'll be coming out any minute to tell us."

"I'm tired, Pop."

"Tired?" With a great, carrying laugh, the man whisked the boy out his chair and into his arms. "This is no time for sleeping, boy. It's a great moment. Another O'Hurley's about to be born. It's opening night."

Trace settled his head on his father's shoulder. "We didn't make it to the theater."

"There's other nights for that." He suffered only a moment's pang over the canceled show. But there were clubs even in Duluth. He'd find a booking or two before they caught the next train.

He'd been born to entertain, to sing, to dance his way through life, and he thanked his lucky stars that his Molly was the same. God knew they didn't make much of a living following the circuit and playing in second-class clubs and smoky lounges, but there was time yet. The big break was always just one show away. "Before you know it, we'll bill ourselves as the Four O'Hurleys. There'll be no stopping us."

"No stopping us," the boy murmured, having heard it all before.

"Mr. O'Hurley?"

Frank stopped. His hands tightened on his son as he turned to the doctor. He was only a man, and terrifyingly ignorant of what went on in childbirth. "I'm O'Hurley." His throat was dry. There wasn't even any spit to swallow. "Molly. Is Molly all right?"

Grinning, the doctor lifted a hand to rub his chin. "Your wife's quite a woman."

Relief came in a wave. Overcome by it, Frank kissed his son hard. "Hear that, boy? Your mom's quite a woman. And the baby. I know it was early, but the baby's all right?"

"Strong and beautiful," the doctor began. "Every one of them."

"Strong and beautiful." Beside himself with joy, Frank went into a quick two-step. "My Molly knows how to have babies. She might get her cues mixed up, but she always comes through like a trouper. Isn't that..." His words trailed off and he stared at the doctor who was continuing to smile at him. "Every one of them?"

"This is your son?"

"Yes, this is Trace. What do you mean every one of them?"

"Mr. O'Hurley, your son has three sisters."

"Three." With Trace still in his arms, Frank sank into the chair. His wiry dancer's legs had turned to water. "*Three* of them. All at once?"

"A couple minutes apart, but three at last count."

He sat a minute, stunned. Three. He hadn't yet figured out how they were going to feed one more. Three. All girls. As the shock wore off, he started to laugh. He'd been blessed with three daughters. Francis O'Hurley wasn't a man who cursed fate. He embraced it.

"You hear that, boy? Your mom's gone and had herself triplets. Three for the price of one. And I'm a man who loves a bargain." Springing up, he grabbed the doctor's hand and pumped it. "Bless you. If there's a man luckier than Francis Xavier O'Hurley tonight, I'm damned if I know him."

"Congratulations."

"You've got a wife?"

"Yes, I do."

"What's her name?"

"It's Abigail."

"Then Abigail it is for one of them. When can I see my family?"

"In just a few minutes. I'll have one of the nurses come down and look after your son."

"Oh, no." Frank caught Trace's hand in his. "He goes with me. It isn't every day a boy gets three sisters."

The doctor started to explain the rules, then caught himself. "Are you as stubborn as your wife, Mr. O'Hurley?"

He poked his slight chest out. "She took lessons from me."

"Come this way."

He saw them first through the glass walls of the nursery, three tiny forms lying in incubators. Two slept, while the other wailed in annoyance. "She's letting the world know she's here. Those are your sisters, Trace."

Awake now, and critical, Trace studied them. "Pretty scrawny."

"So were you, little baboon." The tears came. He was too Irish to be ashamed of them. "I'll do my best for you. For each and every one of you." He placed a hand on the glass and hoped it would be enough somehow.

Chapter One

It wasn't going to be an ordinary day. Now that the decision had been made, it would be a long time before things settled down to the merely ordinary again. She could only hope she was doing the right thing.

In the quiet, animal scented air of the barn, Abby saddled her horse. Maybe it was wrong to steal this time in the middle of the day when there was still so much to be done, but she needed it. An hour alone, away from the house, away from obligations, seemed like an enormous luxury.

Abby hesitated, then shook her head and fastened the cinch. If you were going to steal, you might as well go for the luxurious. Because it was something her father might have said, she laughed to herself. Besides, if Mr. Jorgensen really wanted to buy the foal, he'd call back. The books needed balancing and the feed bill was overdue. She could deal with it later. Right now she wanted a fast ride to nowhere.

Two of the barn cats circled, then settled back into the hay as she led the roan gelding outside. His breath puffed out in a cloud of mist as she double-checked his cinch. "Let's go, Judd." With the ease of long experience, she swung herself into the saddle and headed south.

There would be no fast ride here, where the snow and mud had mixed itself into a slushy mire. The air was cold and heavy with damp, but she felt a sense of anticipation. Things were changing, and wasn't that all anyone could ask? They kept to a fast walk, with both of them straining for what always seemed just out of reach. Freedom.

Perhaps agreeing to be interviewed for this book would bring some portion of it. She could only hope. But the doubts she'd lived with ever since the arrangements had been made still hovered. What was right, what was wrong, what were the consequences? She'd have to assume the responsibility, no matter what occurred.

She rode over the land she loved yet never quite considered her own.

The snow was melting in the pasture. In another month, she thought, the foals could play on the new grass. She'd plant hay and oats, and this year—maybe this year—her books would inch over into the black.

Chuck would never have worried. He'd never thought about tomorrow, only about the next moment. The next car race. She knew why he'd bought the land in rural Virginia. Perhaps she'd always known. But at the time she'd been able to take his gesture of guilt as a gesture of hope. Her ability to find and hold on to thin threads of hope had gotten her through the last eight years.

Chuck had bought the land, then had spent only a few scattered weeks on it. He'd been too restless to sit and watch the grass grow. Restless, careless and selfish, that was Chuck. She'd known that before she'd married him. Perhaps that was why she'd married him. She couldn't claim he'd ever pretended to be anything else. It was simply that she'd looked and seen what she'd wanted to see. He'd swept into her life like the comet he was and, blinded with fascination, she'd followed.

The eighteen-year-old Abigail O'Hurley had been stunned and thrilled at being romanced by the dramatic Chuck Rockwell. His name had been front-page news as he'd raced his way through the Grand Prix circuit. His name had been in bold type on the scandal sheets as he'd raced his way through the hearts of women. The young Abigail hadn't read the tabloids.

He'd spun her into his life in Miami, charmed and dazzled her. He'd offered excitement. Excitement and a freedom from responsibilities. She'd been married before she'd been able to catch her breath.

Though a light drizzle was falling now, Abby stopped her horse. She didn't mind the rain that dampened her face and jacket. It added another quality she'd needed that morning. Isolation. A coward's way, she knew, but she'd never thought herself brave. What she had done—what she would continue to do—was survive.

The land curved gently, patched with snow, misted with a fog that hovered over it. When Judd pawed the ground impatiently, she patted his neck until he was quiet again. It was so beautiful. She'd been to Monte Carlo, to London and Paris and Bonn, but after nearly five years of day-to-day living and dawn-to-dusk working, she still thought this was the most beautiful sight in the world.

The rain splattered down, promising to make the dirt roads that crisscrossed her land all but unmanageable. If the temperatures dropped that night, the rain would freeze and leave a slick and dangerous sheen of ice over the snow. But it was beautiful. She owed Chuck for this. And for so much more.

He'd been her husband. Now she was his widow. Before he'd burned himself out he'd singed her badly, but he'd left her two of the most important things in her life: her sons.

It was for them she'd finally agreed to let the writer come. She'd dodged offers from publishers for more than four years. That hadn't stopped an unauthorized biography of Chuck Rockwell or the stories that still appeared from time to time in the papers. After months of soul-searching, Abby had finally come to the conclusion that if she worked with a writer, a good writer, she would have some control over the final product. When it was done, her sons would have something of their father.

Dylan Crosby was a very good writer. Abby knew that was as much a disadvantage as an advantage. He'd poke into areas she was determined to keep off-limits. She wanted him to. When he did, she'd answer in her way, and she'd finally close that chapter of her life.

She would have to be clever. With a shake of her head she clucked to her horse and sent him moving again. The trouble was, she'd never been the clever one. Chantel had been that. Her older sister—older by two and a half minutes—had always been able to plan and manipulate and make things happen.

Then there was Maddy, her other sister, younger by two minutes and ten seconds. Maddy was the outgoing one, the one who could usually make her own way through sheer drive and will.

But she was Abby, the middle triplet. The quiet one. The responsible one. The dependable one. Those titles still made her wince.

Her problem now wasn't a label that had been pinned on her before she could walk. Her problem now was Dylan Crosby, former investigative reporter turned biographer. In his twenties he'd unearthed a Mafia connection that had eventually crumbled one of the largest mob families on the East Coast. Before he'd turned thirty he'd unhinged the career of a senator with an unreported Swiss bank account and aspirations to higher office. Now she had to handle him.

And she would. After all, he would be on her turf, under her roof. She would feed him information. The secrets she wanted kept secret were locked in her own head and her own heart. She alone had the key.

If she'd learned nothing else as the middle daughter of a pair of road-roving entertainers, she'd learned how to act. To get what she wanted, all she had to do was give Dylan Crosby one hell of a show.

Never tell the whole truth, girl. Nobody wants to hear it. That's what her father would have said. And that, Abby told herself with a smile, was what she'd keep reminding herself of over the next few months.

A bit reluctant to leave the open road and the rain, Abby turned her horse and headed back. It was almost time to begin.

Dylan cursed the rain and reached out the window again to wipe at the windshield with an already-drenched rag. The wiper on his side was working only in spurts. The one on the other side had quit altogether. Icy rain soaked through his coat sleeve as he held the wheel with one hand and cleared his vision with the other. He'd been mad to buy a twenty-five-year-old car, classic or not. The '62 Vette looked like a dream and ran like a nightmare.

It probably hadn't been too smart to drive down from New York in February either, but he'd wanted the freedom of having his own car—such as it was. At least the snow he'd run into in Delaware had turned to rain as he'd driven south. But he cursed the rain again as it pelted through the open window and down his collar.

It could be worse, he told himself. He couldn't think of precisely how; but it probably could. After all, he was finally going to sink his teeth into a project he'd been trying to make gel for three years. Apparently Abigail O'Hurley Rockwell had decided she'd squeezed the publisher for all she could get.

A pretty sharp lady, he figured. She'd snagged one of the hottest and wealthiest race car drivers on the circuit. And she'd hardly been more than a kid. Before she'd reached nineteen she'd been wearing mink and diamonds and rolling dice in places like Monte Carlo. It was never much strain to spend someone else's money. His ex-wife had shown him that in a mercifully brief eighteen-month union.

Women were, after all, born with guile. They were fashioned to masquerade as helpless, vulnerable creatures. Until they had their hooks in you. To shake free, you had to bleed a little. Then if you were smart, you took a hard look at the scars from time to time to remind yourself how life really worked.

Dylan struggled with the map beside him, held it in front while steering with his elbows, then swore again. Yes, that had been his turn. He'd just missed it. With a quick glance up and down the stretch of rain-fogged road, he spun into a U-turn. The wipers might be pitiful, but the Vette knew how to move.

He couldn't imagine the Chuck Rockwell he'd followed and admired choosing to settle in the backwoods of Virginia. Maybe the little woman had talked him into buying it as some sort of hideaway. She'd certainly been hibernating there for the past few years.

Just what kind of woman was she? In order to write a thorough biography of the man, he had to understand the woman. She'd stuck with Rockwell like glue for nearly the first full year on the circuit, then she'd all but disappeared. Maybe the smell of gas and smoking tires had annoyed her. She hadn't been in the stands for her husband's victories or his defeats. Most importantly, she hadn't been there when he'd run his last race. The one that had killed him. From the information Dylan had, she'd finally shown up at the funeral three days later but had hardly spoken a word. She hadn't shed a tear.

She'd married a gold mine and turned a blind eye to his infidelities. Money was the only answer. Now, as his widow, she was in the position of never having to lift a finger. Not bad for a former singer who'd never made it past hotel lounges and second-rate clubs.

He had to slow the Vette to a crawl to make it down the slushy, rut-filled lane marked by a battered mailbox with Rockwell painted on the side.

Obviously she didn't believe in spending much money on maintenance. Dylan wiped his window again and set his teeth against each jarring bump. When he heard his muffler scrape, he stopped cursing the rain and started cursing Abigail. The way he saw it, she had a closetful of silk and fur but wouldn't shell out for minimal road repair.

When he saw the house, he perked up a bit. It wasn't the imposing, oppressive plantation house he'd been expecting. It was charming and homey, right down to the rocker on the front porch. The shutters on the windows were painted Colonial blue, providing a nice contrast to the white frame. A deck with a double railing skirted the second floor. Though he could see the house needed a new paint job, it didn't look run-down, just lived-in. There was smoke trailing up from the chimney and a bike with training wheels leaning on its kickstand under the overhang of the roof. The sound of a dog's deep-throated barking completed the scene.

He'd often thought of finding a place just like this for himself. A place away from crowds and noise where he could concentrate on writing. It reminded him of the home he'd had as a child, where security had gone hand in hand with hard work.

When his muffler scraped the road again, he was no longer charmed. Dylan pulled up behind a pickup truck and a compact station wagon and shut off his engine. Dropping his rag on the floor mat, he rolled up his window and had started to open the door when a mass of wet fur leaped on it.

The dog was enormous. Maybe it had meant to give a friendly greeting, but in its current bedraggled state, the animal didn't look too pleasant. As Dylan gauged its size against that of a small hippo the dog scraped two muddy paws down his window and barked.

"Sigmund!"

Both Dylan and the dog looked toward the house, where a woman stood near the porch steps. So this was Abigail, he mused. He'd seen enough pictures of her over the years to recognize her instantly. The fresh-faced ingenue in the pits at Rockwell's races. The stunning socialite in London and Chicago. The cool, composed widow by her husband's grave. Yet she wasn't precisely what he'd expected.

Her hair, a honey blond, fell across her forehead in wispy bangs and skimmed her shoulders. She looked very slender, and very comfortable in jeans and boots and a bulky sweater that bagged at her hips. Her face was pale and delicate through the rain. He couldn't see the color of her eyes, but he could see her mouth, full and unpainted as she called to the dog again.

"Sigmund, get down now."

The dog let out a last halfhearted bark and obeyed. Cautious, Dylan opened the door and stepped out. "Mrs. Rockwell?"

"Yes. Sorry about the dog. He doesn't bite. Very often."

"There's good news," Dylan muttered, and popped his trunk.

As he pulled out his bags, Abby stood where she was while her nerves tightened. He was a stranger, and she was letting him into her home, into her life. Maybe she should stop it now, right now before he'd taken another step.

Then he turned, bags in hand, and looked at her. Rain streamed from his hair. It was dark, darker now wet and plastered around his face. Not a kind face, she thought immediately as she rubbed her palms on her thighs. There was too much living in it, too much knowledge, for kindness. A woman had to be crazy to let a man like that into her life. Then she saw that his clothes were drenched and his shoes already coated with mud.

"Looks like you could use some coffee."

"Yeah." He gave the dog a last look as it sniffed around his ankles. "Your lane's a mess."

"I know." She gave him a small, apologetic smile as she noted that his car had fared no better than he. "It's been a hard winter."

He didn't step forward. With the rain pelting between them, he stood watching her. Summing her up, Abby decided, and she thrust her nervous hands in her pockets. She'd committed herself, and she wouldn't get what she wanted if she allowed herself to be a coward now.

"Come inside." She went to the door to wait for him.

Her eyes looked dark, a soft green, and if he hadn't known better he'd have said they were frightened. The delicacy he'd seen at a distance became more apparent at close range. She had elegant cheekbones and a slightly pointed chin that gave her face a triangular piquant look. Her skin was pale, her lashes dark. Dylan decided she was either a magician with cosmetics or wasn't wearing any. She smelled of rain and woodsmoke.

Pausing at the door, Dylan pried off his shoes. "I don't think you want me tramping around the place in those."

"I appreciate it." He stepped easily into her house in his stockinged feet while she stood with her hand on the knob feeling desperate and awkward. "Why don't you just leave your things there for now and come into the kitchen? It's warm; you can dry out."

"Fine." He found the inside of the house as unexpected as he'd found the exterior. The floors were worn, their shine a bit dull. He saw on a table by the staircase a crude papier-mâché flower that appeared to have been made by a child. As they walked, Abby bent down to pick two little plastic men in space regalia and continued without breaking rhythm.

"You drove down from New York?"

"Yeah."

"Not a very pleasant ride in this weather."

"No."

He wasn't purposely being rude, though he could be when it suited him. At the moment, the house interested him more than small talk. There were no dishes in the sink, and the floor was scrubbed clean. Nevertheless, the kitchen was hardly tidy. On every available space on the refrigerator door were pictures, drawings, memos. On the breakfast bar was a half-completed jigsaw puzzle. Three and a half pairs of pint-size tennis shoes were jumbled at the back door.

But there was a fire in a brick fireplace, and the scent of coffee.

If he wasn't going to bother to speak to her, they wouldn't get far, Abby mused. She turned for another look. No, his face wasn't kind, but it was intriguing, with its untidy night's growth of beard. His brows were as dark as his hair, and thick over eyes that were a pale green. Intense eyes. She recognized that. Hadn't she been fatally attracted to intensity before? Chuck's eyes had been brown, but the message had been the same. *I get what I want because I don't give a damn what I have to do to win.*

He hadn't. Abby was very much afraid she'd just opened her life to the same kind of man. But she was older now, she reminded herself. Infinitely wiser. And this time she wasn't in love.

"I'll take your coat." She held out her hands and waited until he shrugged out of it. For the first time in years she found herself noticing and reacting to a male body. His was tall and rangy, and a response trickled into her slowly. Abby felt it, recognized it, then put a stop to it. Turning, she hung his coat on a peg by the door. "What do you take in your coffee?"

"Nothing. Just black."

It had always been true for Abby that to keep occupied was to keep calm. She chose an oversize mug for him and a smaller one for herself. "How long have you been on the road?"

"I drove through the night."

"Through the night?" She glanced over her shoulder as he settled at the bar. "You must be exhausted." But he didn't look it. Though he was unkempt, he seemed to be completely alert.

"I got my second wind." He accepted the mug and noticed that her long, narrow hands were ringless. Not even a gold band. When he lifted his eyes, they were cynical. "I'd guess you know how that is."

Lifting a brow, she sat across from him. As a mother, she knew what it was to lose a night's sleep and will herself through the next day. "I guess I do." Since he didn't seem interested in polite conversation, she'd get right down to business. "I've read your work, Mr. Crosby. Your book on Millicent Driscoll was tough, but accurate."

"Accurate's the key word."

She sipped coffee as she watched him. "I can respect that. And I suppose there was enough pity for her from other sources. Did you know her personally?"

"Not until after her suicide." He warmed his hands on the mug as the fire crackled beside him. "I had to get to know her afterward in order to write the book."

"She was a sensational actress, a sensational woman. But her life wasn't an easy one. I knew her slightly through my sister."

"Chantel O'Hurley, another sensational actress."

Abby smiled and softened. "Yes, she is. You met her, didn't you, when you were researching Millicent?"

"Briefly." And there'd been no love lost there. "All three of the O'Hurley triplets seemed to have made their mark . . . one way or the other."

Her eyes met his, calm, accepting. "One way or the other."

"How does it feel having sisters causing ripples on both coasts?"

"I'm very proud of them." The answer came immediately, without any extra shades of meaning.

"No plans to break back into show business yourself?"

She would have laughed if she hadn't detected the cynicism in his voice. "No. I have other priorities. Have you ever seen Maddy on Broadway?"

"Couple of times." He sipped. The coffee was making up for those last few filthy miles of road. "You don't look like her. You don't look like either one of them."

She was used to that, the inevitable comparisons. "No. My father always thought we'd have been a sensation if we'd been identical. More coffee, Mr. Crosby?"

"No, I'm fine. The story goes that Chuck Rockwell walked into that little club where you and your family were playing on a whim, and that he never looked twice at either of your sisters. Only you."

"Is that how the story goes?" Abby pushed her coffee aside and rose.

"Yeah. People generally lean toward the romantic."

"But you don't." She began to busy herself at the stove.

"What are you doing?"

"I'm starting dinner. I hope you like chili."

So she cooked. Or at least she was cooking tonight, perhaps to build some sort of impression. Dylan leaned back in his stool and watched her brown meat. "I'm not writing a romance, Mrs. Rockwell. If the publisher didn't make the ground rules clear to you, I'll do it now."

She concentrated on the task at hand. "Why waste time?"

"I haven't any to waste. First rule is, *I'm* writing this book. That's what I'm paid for. You're paid to cooperate."

Abby added spices with a deft hand. "I appreciate you pointing that out. Are there other rules?"

She was as cool as her reputation indicated. Cool and, a good many had said, unfeeling. "Just this. The book is about Chuck Rockwell; you're a part of it. Whatever I find out about you, however personal, is mine. You gave up your privacy when you signed the agreement."

"I gave up my privacy, Mr. Crosby, when I married Chuck." She stirred the sauce, then added a touch of cooking wine. "Am I wrong, or do you have reservations about writing this book?"

"Not about the book. About you."

She turned to him, and the momentary puzzlement in her eyes vanished as she studied his face. He wouldn't be the first to have come to the conclusion that she'd married Chuck for money. "I see. That's frank enough. Well, it isn't necessary for you to like me."

"No, it isn't. That goes both ways. The one thing I will be with you, Mrs. Rockwell, is honest. I'm going to write the most thorough and comprehensive biography of your husband I can. To do that I'm bound to rub you the wrong way—plenty—before we're done."

She set the lid on the pot, then brought the coffee to the bar with her. "I'm not easily annoyed. I've often been told I'm too...complacent."

"You'll be annoyed before this is over."

After adding more coffee to her mug, she set the pot on a hot pad. "It sounds as though you're looking forward to it."

"I'm not much on smooth water."

This time she did laugh, but it was a quick, almost regretful sound. She lifted her cup. "Did you ever happen to meet Chuck?"

"No."

"You'd have understood each other very well. He was a man with one goal in mind. To win. He'd run the race his way, or not at all. There was very little flexibility."

"And you?"

Though the question was offhand, she took it seriously. "One of my biggest problems growing up was that I'd tend to bend whenever I was asked. I've learned." She finished her coffee. "I'll show you to your room. You can unpack and get your bearings before dinner."

She led him down the hall and took one of his suitcases in hand before he could tell her not to bother. He knew it was heavy, but while he gathered the rest of his things, he watched her carry it easily up the stairs. Stronger than she looked, Dylan mused. It was just one more reason not to take her—or anything about her—at face value.

"There's a bath at the end of the hall. The hot water's fairly reliable." After pushing open a door, she set his case down next to the bed. "I brought a desk up here. I do have a study of sorts downstairs, but I thought this would be more convenient."

"This is fine."

It was more than fine. The room smelled faintly of lemon oil and spice, fresh and inviting. He liked antiques and recognized the Chippendale headboard and the museum-quality shaving stand. There were sprigs of dried weeds mixed with silver-maple twigs in a brass pot on a chest of drawers. The curtains were drawn back to give him a view of rolling, snow-covered hills and a barn whose wood had mellowed to gray.

"It's a nice place."

"Thanks." She looked out the window herself and remembered. "You should have seen it when we bought it. There were probably five spots where the roof didn't leak, and the plumbing was more wish than reality. But I knew it was for me as soon as I saw it."

"You picked it out?" He carried his typewriter to the desk. It was his first order of business.

"Yes."

"Why?"

She was still looking out the window, so her back was toward him. He thought he heard her sigh. "A person needs to sink down roots. At least some people do."

He unearthed his tape recorder and set it next to his typewriter. "A long way from the fast lane."

"I never raced." She looked over her shoulder, then turned, seeing his tools already set out. "Do you have everything you need?"

"For now. One question before we get started, Mrs. Rockwell. Why now? Why after all this time did you agree to authorize a biography of your husband?"

There were two reasons, two very important, very precious reasons, but she didn't think he'd understand. "Let's just say I wasn't ready before. Chuck's been gone for nearly five years now."

And after five years the money might be running out. "I'm sure the deal was lucrative." When she didn't answer, he glanced over. There was no anger in her eyes. He would have preferred it to the cool, unreadable expression that was there.

"Dinner should be ready at six. We keep early hours here."

"Mrs. Rockwell, when I insult you I'm prepared to be kicked back."

She smiled for the first time. It touched her eyes and gave her face a calm, rather sweet vulnerability. He felt a twinge of guilt and a tug of attraction, both unexpected. "I don't fight well. That's why I generally avoid it."

There was a crash outside, but she didn't even jolt. It was followed by a wailing yell worthy of an Indian circling a wagon train. The dog sent up a riot of barking just before something along the lines of an elephant stampede landed on the porch.

"There are fresh towels in the bathroom."

"Thanks. Mind if I ask what that is?"

"What?"

And for the first time he saw real humor in her eyes. The vulnerability was gone. Here was a woman who knew who she was and where she was going. "It sounds like an invasion."

"That's just what it is." She crossed the room, then paused when the front door slammed open, then shut, shaking the pictures on the walls.

"Mom! We're home!"

The greeting echoed, followed by another riot of crashing feet and the beginnings of a heated argument. "My children always feel as though they have to announce themselves. God knows why. If you'll excuse me, I have to try to save the living room carpet."

With that, she left him alone with his thoughts.

Chapter Two

By the time she got to the kitchen, her sons were shedding their outdoor clothes. She'd followed the thin stream of water from the front door.

"Hi, Mom." Both boys grinned at her. School was out and the world was beautiful.

"Hi, yourself." A few damp books sat on the bar. A small puddle was forming in front of the refrigerator where the two boys stood. The door was wide open and the cool air vied with the heat from the fire. Abby surveyed the damage and found it minimal. "Chris, that looks like your coat on the floor."

Her youngest glanced around in apparent surprise. "Tommy Harding got in trouble on the bus again." He gathered up his coat and hung it on one of the lower hooks by the rear door. "He has to sit up in the front for two whole weeks."

"He spit at Angela," Ben announced with relish as he got a sturdy grip on a jug of juice. "Right in her hair."

"Lovely." Abby picked up Chris's dripping gloves and handed them to him. "I don't suppose you had anything to do with it."

"Uh-uh." Juice sloshed, but Ben made it to the counter. "I just said she was ugly."

"She's only a little ugly." Chris, always ready to root for the underdog, busied himself with his boots.

"Toad face," Ben stated as he poured juice in a glass. "Chris and I raced from the bus. I gave him a head start, but I still won."

"Congratulations."

"I almost won." Chris struggled with his second boot. "And I got awful hungry."

"One cookie."

"I mean *awful* hungry."

He had the face of a cherub, round, pale and pretty. His blond hair curled a bit around his ears, and his hazel eyes were luminous as he looked up at her. Abby relented with a sigh. "Two." He was going to be a heartbreaker.

"I'm starving." Ben gulped down his juice, then swiped the back of his hand across his mouth. Her little heathen. His hair was already darkening from blond to a sandy brown and fell every which way around his face. His eyes were dark and wicked.

"Two," Abby told him, accepting the fact that they knew each other's measure. She was boss. For now.

Ben dipped his hand in a cookie jar shaped like a duck. "Whose car's out front? It's neat."

"The writer, remember?" Going to the closet, Abby took out a mop and began to scrub quickly at the water on the floor. "Mr. Crosby."

"The guy who's going to write the book about our dad?"

"That's right."

"Don't see why anybody'd want to read about somebody who's dead."

There it was again, Abby thought. Ben's frank and careless dismissal of his father. Was Chuck to blame for it, or was she at fault for refusing to carry her child papoose-style around the circuit? Blame didn't matter, she decided. Only the result.

"Your father was very well-known, Ben. People still admire him."

"Like George Washington?" Chris asked, stuffing the last of his cookie in his mouth.

"Not exactly. You two should go up and change before dinner. And don't disturb Mr. Crosby," she added. "He's in the spare room nearest the stairs. He had a long drive, and he's probably resting."

"'Kay." Ben sent Chris a significant look behind their mother's back. "We'll be real quiet."

"I appreciate it." Abby waited until they were gone, then leaned on the mop handle. She was doing the right thing, she told herself again. She had to be.

"Don't make the stairs creak," Ben warned and started up in a pattern he'd discovered a few months before. "He'll know we're coming."

"We're not supposed to bother him." But Chris meticulously followed his brother's path.

"We're not gonna. We're just going to look at him."

"But Mom said—"

"Listen." Ben paused dramatically three steps from the top, keeping his voice to a whisper. "Suppose he isn't a writer really. Suppose he's a robber."

Chris's eyes widened. "A robber?"

"Yeah." Warming to the theme, Ben bent close to his brother's ear. "He's a robber and he's going to wait until we're all sleeping tonight. Then he's going to clean us out."

"Is he going to take my trucks?"

"Probably." Then Ben played his ace. "I bet he has a gun, too. So we've gotta be real quiet and just watch him."

Sold, Chris nodded. The two boys, hearts thumping, crept up the last steps.

With his hands tucked in his back pockets, Dylan stood looking out the window. The hills weren't so different from the hills he'd seen out of his bedroom window as a boy. The rain pelted down, the fog rolled. There wasn't another house in sight.

Unexpected. But then, he preferred the unexpected. He'd thought Abigail O'Hurley Rockwell's home would have been a showplace of the ornate and the elegant. He'd been certain he'd find a houseful of servants. Unless they were out on errands, she didn't appear to have any at all, and her house was simply comfortable.

He'd known, of course, that she had children, but he'd expected nannies or boarding school. The woman whose picture he had in his file, dressed in white mink and glittering with diamonds, wouldn't have the time or inclination to actually raise children.

If she wasn't that woman, who the hell was she? It was his job to research the life of Chuck Rockwell, but Dylan found himself more interested in the widow.

Hardly looked like a widow, he mused as he moved to drop one of his suitcases on the bed. Looked more like a graduate student on winter break. But then she had been an actress of sorts. Perhaps she still was.

He flipped back the top of his suitcase. A small sound, hardly more than a murmur, caught his attention. As an investigative reporter, Dylan had found himself in enough back alleys and seedy bars to develop eyes in the back of his head. Casually he pulled out a stack of shirts and sweaters while he shifted his gaze to the mirror at the foot of the bed.

The bedroom door opened slowly, just a crack, then a tiny bit wider. He tensed and waited, though it appeared as though he simply continued to unpack. He saw two eyes in the mirror one above the other. Moving to the dresser, he heard the sound of nervous breathing. When the door opened a bit wider, he saw small fingers wrap around the edge.

"He looks like a robber." Ben said in a piercing whisper, hardly able to contain the excitement. "He's got shifty eyes."

"Do you think he's got a gun?"

"Probably a whole arsenal." Wildly pleased, Ben followed Dylan's movements around the room. "He's going to the closet," he whispered frantically. "Be quiet."

The words were hardly out of his mouth when the door was yanked open. The two boys tumbled into the room.

Sprawled on the carpet, Chris looked up at the man's face, which seemed miles above his. His bottom lip poked out, but his eyes were dry. "You can't have my trucks." He was ready to yell frantically for his mother at a moment's notice.

"Okay." Amused, Dylan crouched down until they were almost eye-to-eye. "Maybe I could see them sometime."

Chris's eyes darted back to his brother. "Maybe. Are you a robber?"

"Chris!" Mortified, Ben struggled to untangle himself from his brother and stand. "He's just a kid."

"Am not. I'm six."

"Six." Dylan struggled to look suitably impressed. "And you?"

"I'm eight." Ben's conscience tugged at him. "Well, I will be pretty soon. Mom thinks you're a writer."

"Sometimes I think so, too." A good-looking boy, Dylan decided, and with such an eager gleam of curiosity in his eyes he was hard to resist. "I'm Dylan." He held out his hand and waited while Ben pondered.

"I'm Ben." He took Dylan's hand, appreciating the man-to-man offer. "This is Chris."

"Nice to meet you." Dylan offered his hand to Chris. With a sheepishly pleased smile, he took it.

"We thought your car was neat."

"It has its moments."

"Ben said it probably goes two hundred miles an hour."

"It might." Unable to resist, he ruffled the boy's hair. "I don't."

Chris grinned. He liked the way the man smelled, so different from his mom. "My mom said we weren't supposed to disturb you."

"Did she?" Dylan set the boy on his feet, then rose himself. "I'll let you know when you do."

Accepting the words at face value, Chris climbed onto the bed and chattered while Dylan unpacked. Ben held back, saying little and watching everything.

Doesn't trust easily, Dylan thought. Though he agreed with the sentiment, he thought it was a pity to find it in such a small boy. The little one was a crackerjack, and one who'd believe whatever tumbled out of your mouth. It would pay to watch what you said.

Chris watched as Dylan pulled out a carton of cigarettes. "Mom says those are a dirty habit."

Dylan tossed them into a dresser drawer. "Moms are pretty smart."

"Do you like dirty habits?"

"I..." Dylan decided to let that one ride. "Why don't you hand me that camera?"

Willing to please, Chris drew the compact 35-millimeter out of the case. He held it for just a moment, eyeing the knobs. "It's pretty neat."

"Thanks."

"You going to take our picture?"

"I just might." As he set in on the dresser, Dylan glanced in the mirror and saw Ben poking gingerly at his tape recorder. "Interested?"

Caught, Ben snatched his hands back. "Spies use these."

"So I've heard. Got any around here?"

Ben sent him a quietly measuring look he wouldn't have expected from a boy twice his age. "Maybe."

"We thought Mr. Petrie who helps with the horses was a spy for awhile." Chris looked in the suitcase to see if there was anything else interesting. "But he wasn't."

"You have horses?"

"We got a bunch of them."

"What kind?"

Chris shrugged. "Mostly big ones."

"You're such a dope," Ben said. "They're Morgans. One day I'm going to ride Thunder, that's the stallion.'' As he spoke, the caution in his eyes vanished, to be replaced by enthusiasm. ''He's the best there is.''

So this was the key to the boy, Dylan mused, that someone could turn if he cared to. ''I had a Tennessee walker when I was a kid. Sixteen hands.''

''Sixteen?'' Ben's eyes widened before he remembered he shouldn't be too enthusiastic. ''He probably wasn't as fast as Thunder.'' When Dylan made no comment, Ben struggled, then gave up. ''What'd you call him?''

''Sly. He had a way of knowing which pocket you had the carrot in.''

''Ben. Chris.''

Ben flushed with guilt as he spotted his mother in the doorway. She had that look in her eye. Oblivious, Chris bounced happily on the bed. ''Hi, Mom. I don't think Dylan's a robber after all.''

''I'm sure we're all relieved to hear that. Benjamin, didn't I tell you not to disturb Mr. Crosby?''

''Yes, ma'am.'' You had to use ''ma'am'' when she used ''Benjamin.''

''They weren't.'' Dylan took a pair of slacks and hung them in the closet. ''We were getting acquainted.''

''That's kind of you.'' She sent him an even look, then ignored him. ''Maybe you boys have forgotten about your chores?''

''But, Mom—''

She cut Ben off with a look. ''I don't think we have to discuss responsibilities again.''

Dylan stuck a shirt in his drawer and tried not to chuckle. He'd heard the same line in the same tone from his own mother countless times.

"You have animals depending on you for their dinner," Abby reminded her sons. "And—" she rustled a paper "—this seems to have fallen on the floor. I'm sure you were going to show it to me."

Ben shuffled his feet as she held up his C in spelling. "I sort of studied."

"Mmm." Walking over, she cupped his chin in her hand. "Delinquent."

He smiled, knowing the crisis had passed. "I'm going to study tonight."

"You bet you are. Now scram. You too." She held out a hand for Chris as Ben scrambled from the room.

"Ben said he might steal my trucks."

Abby lifted him up by the elbows to kiss him soundly. "You're very gullible."

"Is that okay?"

"For now. Change your clothes."

At six, Chris couldn't have defined charm—but he knew he had it. "I'm still *awful* hungry."

"I guess we could eat a little early. If you get your chores done."

Since it seemed cookies were out, he wiggled down and walked to the door. He stopped and aimed a smile at Dylan. "Bye."

"See you."

Abby waited a moment, then turned back. "I'm sorry. I'm afraid they're used to having the run of the house and don't think about other people's privacy.

"They didn't bother me."

She laughed and tossed her hair back from her shoulder. "That won't last, I promise you. If you don't mind, we'll eat when they've finished their chores and cleaned up."

"Anytime."

"Mr. Crosby." The laughter was gone, and her eyes were calm and sober again. But it was her mouth, he realized, that drew his attention. It was full, sensual, serious. "I'm going to try to give you my cooperation with this project. That doesn't include my children."

He drew his shaving kit out of the case. "Which means?"

"I don't want them involved. You aren't to interview or question them about their father."

After setting the kit on his dresser, he turned back to her. Soft. She was a woman who looked soft as butter and she had a voice to match, but he had a feeling she'd grow talons if her children were threatened. That was fair enough. "I hadn't really given that any thought. I'd think both of them a little young to remember much."

You'd be surprised, she thought, but nodded. "Then we understand each other."

"Not yet. Not by a long shot . . . Mrs. Rockwell."

She didn't care for the look in his eyes. It was too . . . intrusive. How much of herself would she have left when he finished his assignment? It was a gamble, and she'd already decided to take it. "I'll have one of the boys let you know when dinner's ready."

After she'd closed the door and started down the hall, she found herself chilled, so chilled that she rubbed her hands up and down her arms. She wanted to call her family, to hear her parents' comforting voices. Or Chantel's caustic one. She dragged a hand through her hair as she walked down the steps. Maybe she could call Maddy and absorb some of her carelessly upbeat views on life in general. She couldn't call Trace. Big brother was roaming his way through Europe or Africa or God knew where.

She couldn't call any of them, Abby reminded herself as she stepped into the kitchen again. She was on her own and had been for years, by her own choice. They'd come, any and all of them would come if she so much as hinted at need. So she couldn't call. She wasn't simply the middle triplet now. She was Abby Rockwell, mother of two sons. She had to see to them, provide for them, raise them. And by God, she was going to make certain they had some kind of legacy from their father.

She pulled vegetables out of the crisper and began to prepare a salad both her sons would mutter over.

When the stock was fed and hands and faces reluctantly washed, Abby turned off the flame under the pot of chili. "Chris, go up and tell Mr. Crosby dinner's ready."

"I'll do it." Ben's offer was quick and out of character. When Abby sent him a questioning look, he shrugged. "I want to get something upstairs anyway."

"All right, thanks. But no fooling around. Everything's ready."

"I don't have to eat mushrooms, do I?" Chris was already pulling himself onto his stool.

"No, you don't have to eat any mushrooms."

"You gonna pick them out?"

"Yes."

"All of them. If I eat one, I'll throw up."

"Understood," she said, and glanced up to see Dylan and Ben come in. "Go ahead and sit, I'm just setting things up." Moving automatically, she began to dish salad into bowls.

"I don't want any," Ben told her as he slid onto his stool.

"Your body does." She added dressing. "Here, Chris, not one mushroom."

"If there is I'm gonna—"

"Yes, I know." She dished up a third bowl and set it in front of Dylan. "Now if you'll—" She caught herself when she glanced over and saw him grinning at her. "Oh, I'm sorry." She looked down at the salad she'd fixed him just as tidily as she had fixed her sons'. "I guess I'm just used to dishing it up."

"It's all right." He picked up a bottle of dressing and shook it lazily. "I think we can handle it from here."

She sat down and began to eat as Chris chattered between and during mouthfuls. Ben was picking at his salad and watching Dylan out of the corner of his eye. Odd, she thought, he looked...what? Wary? Resentful? She couldn't be sure. He wasn't the most open child, but...

Then it occurred to her all at once that Dylan was sitting in what had been Chuck's seat. True, he'd only sat there a handful of times, and those times had been few and far between, but it had been his. Did Ben remember? He'd been barely three the last time his father had stayed at the house. Barely three, she thought, and yet so stiffly adult in too many ways. She felt the elbow nudge her ribs and blinked herself back.

"What?"

Ben pushed his salad bowl aside. "I said I ate most of it."

"Oh." She started to reach for the ladle to spoon out chili.

"I can get it myself."

She started to serve him then caught Dylan's eyes over Ben's head. Something in them made her pass Ben the pot and sit back, annoyed with herself. "The rain seems to be letting up," she commented as she offered the chili to Dylan.

"Seems to." Dylan helped himself. "I guess things'll be a mess for the next few days."

"Mud up to your ankles." Abby set Chris's chili next to him to cool. "If you like being outdoors, I hope you brought something more substantial than your tennis shoes."

"I'll get by." He tasted the chili. Either it was delicious or he was starving. Whatever the reason he dug in. "The boys tell me you have some horses."

"Yes, we breed Morgans. Use your napkin, Chris."

"Breed?" Dylan deftly avoided being splattered with sauce as Chris jiggled his bowl. "I didn't know you were in business."

"Unfortunately, a lot of people don't." Then she smiled and tugged at Ben's ear. "But they will. Do you know anything about horses?"

"He had a rocker," Chris piped up.

"A walker." Ben rolled his eyes and would have wiped his mouth on his sleeve if he hadn't caught the warning look from his mother. "He said it was sixteen hands."

"Did he?"

"I was raised on a farm in Jersey."

"Seems stupid to be a writer, then," Ben commented as he scraped the bottom of his bowl. "Must be boring, like being in school all the time."

"Some people actually enjoy using their minds. More, Mr. Crosby?"

"A little." He took another scoop. Though he wasn't a talkative man, preferring to listen, he found himself compelled to justify his profession to the boy. "You know, when I write I get to travel a lot and meet a lot of people."

"That's pretty good." Ben made patterns on the bottom of his bowl with his fork. "I'm going to travel, too. When I grow up I'm going to be a space marauder."

"Interesting choice," Dylan murmured.

"Then I can fly from galaxy to galaxy and loot and pil...pil..."

"Pillage," Abby finished for him. "Ben's fond of crime. I've already started saving up bail money."

"It's better than Chris. He wants to be a garbage man."

"Not anymore." The fire was in Chris's eyes as he talked through his last mouthful of chili.

"Don't talk with your mouth full, love." She scooted Ben's milk in front of him as a reminder. "We visited Maddy in New York last year. Chris was fascinated with the garbage trucks."

"Dumb." Ben's voice dripped with scorn as he looked at his brother. "Real dumb."

"Ben, isn't it your turn to wash up?"

"Aw, Mom."

"We made an agreement. I cook, you guys take turns with the dishes."

He sulked a moment, but then a wicked gleam appeared in his eyes. "He's living here now." With a jerk of his head, Ben indicated Dylan. "He should have a turn, too."

Why was it, Abby wondered, that Ben was only logical when it was to his advantage? "Ben, Mr. Crosby is a guest. Now—"

"The kid has a point." Dylan spoke casually, but he was rewarded by a grin of approval from Ben. "Since

I'm going to be around a while, the least I can do is follow the rules.''

"Mr. Crosby, you don't have to humor the monsters around here. Ben will be glad to do the dishes."

"No, I won't," he muttered.

"You know, when someone cooks you a good meal, the least you can do is pitch in and clean up the mess." As he pushed away from the counter, Dylan saw Ben hang his head. "I'll take the shift tonight."

Ben's head came up immediately. "No fooling?"

"Seems fair to me."

"Great. Come on, Chris, let's go—"

"Do your homework," Abby finished. She watched Ben's mouth open and close. He knew better than to press his luck. "Then you can watch television." With a clatter of feet, they were down the hall and racing up the stairs. "Such unpretentious children," she murmured. "I suppose I should apologize for their lack of manners again."

"Don't bother. I was a kid once myself."

"I suppose you were." With her elbows on the counter, Abby dropped her chin onto her hands and looked at him. "It's difficult to imagine certain people being small and vulnerable. Would you like anything else, Mr. Crosby?"

"Your kids don't have any problem with my first name. We've had a meal together now, and we're going to be together for a number of weeks. Why don't we try something a little less formal? Abigail?"

"Abby," she corrected automatically.

"Abby." He liked the pretty, old-fashioned sound of it. "It suits you better."

"Dylan's an unusual name."

"My father wanted something solid, like John. My mother was more romantic, and more stubborn."

He was staring at her again in that cool unblinking way she'd already determined meant questions were forming. She wasn't ready to start answering them yet. "My parents always preferred the unusual," she began as she slid off the stool to stack dishes.

"That's my job."

Abby continued to clear the bar. "I'm sure you've earned Ben's undying gratitude for getting him off the hook. But you don't have to feel obligated." She turned with a stack of bowls in her hands and all but ran into him.

"A deal's a deal," he said very quietly, and reached out to take the bowls from her. Their fingers brushed, as lightly as fingers brush every day in ordinary situations. Abby jerked back and nearly sent the dishes crashing to the floor.

"A little jumpy?" He watched her. He had discovered that you learned more from faces than from words.

"I'm not used to having anyone else in the kitchen." A feeble excuse, and one that didn't ring true even to herself. "I'd better give you a hand, at least tonight, until you learn where things go. There's a dishwasher." She grabbed more dishes from the counter, filling her hands and her mind with ordinary chores. "It seems ridiculous that the boys make such a fuss over the dishes when they don't have to do much more than load and unload."

"We could spread out the pain a little more if I cooked once a week and you cleared up."

She was bent over the dishwasher, and she had to straighten to stare at him. "You cook?"

He nudged her aside. "Surprised?"

It was silly to be, she knew. But none of the men in her life had ever known one end of the stove from another. She remembered her father quite clearly hard-boiling eggs on a hot plate in a motel room, but that was as far as it had gone. "I suppose when you live alone, it helps."

He thought of his marriage. She heard him laugh, but he didn't sound amused. "Even when you don't, it helps." The dishwasher rattled a bit as he added dishes. "This thing's a little shaky."

She frowned at the back of his head. "It works." She wasn't about to admit that she'd bought it secondhand and, with a lot of sweat and skinned knuckles, installed it herself.

"You'd know best." With the last of the dishes in, he closed it. "But it sounds to me like a couple of the bolts have shaken loose. You might want to have it looked at."

There were a lot of things that needed to be looked at. And they would be, once the manuscript was submitted and the rest of the advance was in her bank account. "I imagine you want to work out some sort of schedule."

"Eager to start?"

Abby went to the coffeepot and poured two cups without asking. "You're here to get background, I'm here to give it to you. The best times for me are mid-morning or early afternoon, but I'll try to be flexible."

"I appreciate it." He took the coffee, then leaned on the stove, close to her, as a kind of test for both of them. He thought he could just smell the rain on her hair. She stood very still for a moment, still enough that he could see his own reflection in her eyes. When he saw it, he forgot to look for anything else. Incredibly, he found he wanted to reach out, to touch the hair that brushed her shoulders. She stepped back. The reflection vanished, and so did the need.

"Breakfast is early." Concentrate on routine, Abby warned herself. As long as she did, there wouldn't be room for these sudden, sharp desires to sneak up on her. "The kids have to catch the school bus at 7:30, so if you're a late sleeper you're on your own."

"I'll manage."

"If I'm not in the house, I'm probably in the barn or one of the other outbuildings, but I should be ready for you by ten."

And what in hell did a woman with hands like a harpist do in a barn for an hour and a half in the morning? He decided to find out for himself rather than ask. "We'll figure on ten. The time element might vary from day to day."

"Yes, I understand that." The tension was draining as they focused in on business. Abby relaxed against the counter and savored what would be her last cup of coffee for the night. There were hours yet to fill between this and the cup of herbal tea she'd pamper herself with at bedtime. "I'll do the best I can. The evenings, of course, are taken up with the children. They go to bed at 8:30, so if there's something important we can go over it after that. But generally I do my paperwork at night."

"So do I." She had a lovely face, soft, warm, open, with just a touch of reserve around the mouth. It was the kind of face that could make a man forget about feminine guile if he wasn't careful. Dylan was a careful man. "Abby, one question."

"Off-the-record?"

"This time. Why'd you give up show business?"

This time she really laughed. It was low and smooth, a distinctly sensuous sound. "Did you ever happen to catch our act? The O'Hurley Triplets, I mean."

"No."

"I didn't think so. If you had, you wouldn't ask."

It was difficult to resist people who could laugh at themselves. "That bad?"

"Oh, worse. Much worse." Taking her cup to the sink, she rinsed it out. "I have to go up and check on the boys. When they're this quiet for this long, I get antsy. Help yourself to more coffee. The TV's in the living room."

"Abby." He wasn't satisfied with her, with the house, with the situation. Nothing was precisely what it seemed, that much he was sure of. Still, when she turned toward him, her eyes were calm. "I intend to get to the bottom of you," he murmured.

She felt a little jolt inside, but quickly smoothed it over. "I'm not as complex as you seem to want to believe. In any case, you're here to write about Chuck."

"I'm going to do that, too."

That was what she was counting on. That was what she was afraid of. With a nod, she walked out to go to her children.

Chapter Three

For the second time, Dylan heard his door creak open. In bed, abruptly awake, it took him only a moment to remember he wasn't in some hotel room on assignment. Those days were over, and the gun he'd kept under his pillow for three years running wasn't there. Out of habit, he kept his eyes closed and his breathing even.

"Still sleeping." The quiet, slightly disdainful whisper was Ben's.

Chris jockeyed for position and a better view. "How come he gets to sleep late?"

"'Cause he's grown-up, stupid. They get to do whatever they want."

"Mom's up. She's a grown-up."

"That's different. She's a mom."

"Ben, Chris." Dylan judged the low call to be coming from the bottom of the stairs. "Let's move it. The bus'll be here in ten minutes."

"Come on." Ben narrowed his eyes for one last look. "We can spy on him later."

When the door closed, Dylan opened his eyes. He couldn't claim to be an expert on kids, but he was beginning to think that the Rockwell boys were a different kettle of fish altogether. So was their mother. Pushing himself up, he glanced at his watch. 7:20. It seemed things ran on time around here. And it was time he began.

Twenty minutes later, Dylan walked downstairs. The house was quiet. And empty, he decided before he came to the bottom landing. The scent of coffee drew him to the kitchen. It looked as though a hurricane had struck and moved on.

There were two cereal boxes on the breakfast bar, both open, with a trail of puffed wheat and little oat circles leading to the edge. A half-open bag of bread lay on the counter between the sink and stove. Next to it was a good-sized dollop of what Dylan assumed to be grape jelly. There was a jar of peanut butter with the top sitting crookedly and an assortment of knives, spoons and bowls. Muddy paw prints ran just inside the back door, then stopped abruptly.

Didn't get far, did you? Dylan thought as he searched out a cup for coffee. With the first swallow of caffeine rushing through his system, he walked to the window. However confused things looked inside, outside seemed peaceful enough. The rain had frozen and covered what was left of the snow with a shiny, brittle layer. It glistened as the sun shone brightly. By the end of the day, he decided, it would be a mess. Without the fog, he could see past the barn to the rolling hills beyond. If she had neighbors, he thought, they were few and far between. What made a woman bury herself like this? he wondered. Especially a woman who was used to lights and action.

There was something else that bothered him, something that had been bothering him all along. Where were the men in her life? He took another sip, letting his gaze sweep over paddock and outbuildings. Surely a woman who looked like Abby had them. She'd been a widow for four years. A young, wealthy widow. Though he was willing to concede that she took motherhood seriously, that hardly answered the question. Two boys under ten didn't make up for male companionship.

For some reason, she seemed to want him to take her little farm and her domesticity at face value. His mouth twisted in a grimace and he downed the rest of the coffee. He took nothing at face value. Particularly not women.

Then he saw her. She came out of a little shed and closed the door carefully behind her. Her hair caught the sunlight as she combed her fingers through it and just stood there. Her coat was bundled up to her chin and stopped just short of her hips, where slim jeans ran down and tucked into scarred boots.

Was she posing? he thought as a rush of arousal pushed, unwanted, into his system. Did she know he was there, watching as she stood with her face lifted to the sun and a quiet smile on her face? But she never glanced toward the house. She never turned. Swinging the bucket she carried, she walked across the frozen ground to the barn.

Abby had always liked the feel and scents of a barn, especially in the morning, when the animals were just stirring from sleep. The lights was dim, the air a bit musty. She heard the purring of the barn cats as they woke for breakfast. After setting the bucket beside the door, she switched on the lights and began her morning routine.

"Hello, baby." Opening the first stall, she stepped inside to check the chestnut mare, which was nearly ready to foal. "I know, you feel fat and ugly." She chuckled as the mare blew into her hand. "I've felt that way a couple times myself." Gently, expertly, she ran her hands along the mare's belly. The mare's muscles quivered, then relaxed as Abby murmured to her. "In a week or two it'll all be over, then you'll have such a pretty baby. You know Mr. Jorgensen's interested in buying your foal." With a sigh, she rested her cheek against the mare's neck. "Why does that make me feel like a slave trader?"

"First sale?"

She hadn't heard Dylan come in. She turned slowly, one arm still slung around the mare's neck. He'd shaved, and though his face was smooth now, and still attractive, it seemed no kinder to her than before. "Yeah. Up until now I've just been buying and setting up."

He stepped inside to get a closer look. The mare was beautiful, strong and full-bodied in the way of Morgans, with alert eyes and a glossy coat. "You pick this mare out?"

"Eve. I call her Eve because she's the first of my breeders. She was just weaned when I got her at auction. Mr. Petrie said to bid on her, so I bid."

"Looks like your Petrie knows his horseflesh. I'd say this little lady's going to give you plenty of foals. Plan to breed her back?"

"That's the idea." Eve nuzzled into her shoulder. "It doesn't seem fair."

"That's what she's built for." It had been a long time since he'd been around horses. He'd forgotten how good a barn could smell, how soothing it could be to work around and with animals. Maybe people had consumed him for too long. The mare shifted. Abby shifted with her and brushed against him. The contact was anything but soothing. "How many do you have?"

Her mind, usually so orderly, was blank. "How many?"

"Horses."

"Oh." She was being ridiculous, reacting as though she'd never touched a man before. "Eight—the stallion, two mares already bred and two we'll breed in the spring, three geldings for riding." The last was a luxury she'd never regretted. "Not exactly the big leagues," Abby went on, relaxing again.

"Four mares and a decent stallion, properly managed, sounds like a pretty good start to me."

"That's what I've got." She scratched the mare between the ears. "A start."

He watched her reach for a halter. "What are you doing?"

"They need to go out in the paddock while I clean the stalls."

"You? Alone?"

She went to the next stall to repeat the process on a second mare. "Mr. Petrie comes by three times a week to help out, but he's down with the flu like half the county. Come on, girls." Taking the two lead ropes she led the horses out.

For a moment Dylan just stood there with his hands in his pockets. The woman looked to him as though she'd keel over after one shovelful of manure. What was she trying to prove? The martyr act might work on certain men, but he'd always believed that if you asked for it, you probably deserved it.

Then he looked down the line of stalls. He swore as he pulled a halter down. Whether she was doing all this for his benefit or not, he couldn't just stand around and let her work alone.

Outside, Abby closed the paddock gate behind the first two mares, then turned to see Dylan leading out another pair. "Thanks." She met him halfway and automatically reached for the rope. When he just looked at her, she stepped back, feeling foolish. "Look, that wasn't a hint. I don't want you to feel obligated."

"I don't." He walked past her and released the horses in the paddock.

"Mr. Crosby—" she corrected herself "—Dylan. I can handle things. I'm sure you have other things you'd rather do with your morning."

He closed the gate. "Off the top of my head I can only think of about two dozen. Let's get the others."

She lifted her brow, then fell into step beside him. "Well, since you're being so gracious about it."

"I'm known for being gracious."

"I don't doubt it. The geldings go out, the first three stalls on this side. I leave the stallion in until the rest is dealt with. He's apt to bite one of the geldings or mount any mare than isn't fast enough to get away."

"Sounds like a sweetheart."

"He's as mean as they come, but his line's just as pure." As she slipped a halter around a roan, the horse lowered his head, then shoved her hard. Instinctively Dylan made a grab to right her, but she was shoving the horse back and laughing. "Bully," she said accusingly, burying her face in his mane. "He'd rather be taken for a ride than go into the paddock. Maybe later, fella, I've got my hands full today."

When the horses were settled, Abby pulled on a pair of work gloves. "Sure?" she asked as she offered a second pair to Dylan.

"You take the left side." He grabbed a pitchfork and went to work, figuring he'd have the four stalls cleaned out and spread with fresh hay before she'd finished the first.

It had been a while since he'd indulged in pure manual labor. Workouts kept his body in tune but didn't, he discovered, give the same kind of gratification. His muscles coiled and tensed. As the wheelbarrow filled, he rolled it to the rear of the barn and added to the pile. Abby had switched on a portable radio and was singing along as she worked. He ignored her. Or tried to.

She'd never worked alongside a man before. Oh, there was Mr. Petrie, she thought as she wiped a light film of sweat from her brow. But he was different. Chuck had never so much as lifted a hoof pick in the barn. And her father... Abby grinned as she spread fresh hay. Whenever Francis Xavier O'Hurley visited the farm, he always found something vital to do when there was work. One mustn't forget the man was an artist, Abby reminded herself, trying not to think of just how much she missed him and the rest of her family.

The little farm in Virginia didn't suit their life-styles. It hadn't suited Chuck's. It suited her, and it suited her children. That was something she'd never forget. Whatever compromises she had made, whatever compromises she had yet to make, she wouldn't bend there.

Dylan sent his pitchfork into the soiled hay, then glanced up when Abby moved to the stall beside him. "Why don't you finish over there?"

"I already did." She started shoveling.

Dylan glanced over his shoulder, then turned completely around. The three stalls were clean and fresh. Frowning, he turned back. He'd barely started on his third. "You work fast," he muttered.

"It's routine." Because she'd never really understood the male ego, she didn't give it a thought as she filled the wheelbarrow behind them.

"I said I'd do this side."

"Yeah, I appreciate the help." Abby tossed in a last forkful, then walked over to grasp the handles of the wheelbarrow.

"Put that down."

"It's pretty full. I'd just as soon make an extra trip as—"

"Put the damn thing down." He sliced his pitchfork down in the hay and walked toward her. Anger—male anger. Though she hadn't been around it in a good many years, she still recognized it. Cautiously Abby lowered the cart and released the handles.

"All right, it's down."

"I'm not having you haul that thing while I'm around."

"But I—"

"You're not hauling twenty pounds of horse manure while I'm around." He grasped the handles himself. "Understand?"

"Possibly." Calm, patient, Abby picked up her pitchfork again and leaned on it. "I can haul it all I want when you're not around?"

"That's fine." He began to roll it down the sloping concrete.

"That's silly," she said. He muttered something she couldn't quite catch. Shaking her head, she walked outside to begin leading the horses back.

After the one outburst, they worked in silence. As Dylan finished up, Abby returned all the horses to their stalls and fed them. Then only the stallion remained.

"I'll take him out." Abby held a halter behind her back and opened only the top half of the stall door first. "He's moody and unpredictable. Don't care much for being closed up, do you, Thunder?" she murmured, cautiously opening the bottom half and stepping inside. He danced back, eyeing her, but she continued to talk. "In the spring you can just graze and graze. And have your way with those two pretty mares." She slipped the halter around his neck, taking a firm hold as he swung his head in annoyance.

"High-strung," Dylan commented.

"To say the least. Better stand back. He likes to kick, and he isn't particular who."

Taking her at her word, Dylan moved aside. Thunder started to rear, then subsided when Abby scolded him. Scolded him in much the same way, Dylan thought as she continued out of the barn, as he'd heard her scold her sons. He picked up his pitchfork and put his back into it. When Abby came back in, he was nearly done.

"You don't seem to be a stranger to this sort of work." Because he'd shed his coat, she could see the muscles rippling along his forearms. He grunted an answer, but she didn't hear. She wondered what it would feel like to touch those arms when they were flexed with strength. It had been so long, so incredibly long since...

She caught herself and stepped away to stroke one of the mares which was busily gobbling grain.

"Did you raise horses?"

"Cows." Dylan spread hay over the floor of the stall. "We had a dairy farm, but there were always a couple of horses around. I haven't mucked out a stall since I was sixteen."

"Doesn't look like you've forgotten how."

No, he hadn't forgotten how. And it wouldn't be wise to forget what he'd come for. Still, at the moment, he wanted to finish what he'd started. "Got a broom?"

"It's Ben's job to sweep the barn." She took the pitchfork from him and set it on its hook. "I usually leave Thunder out in the paddock through the morning unless it's filthy out, so we're done for now. The least I can do after you saved me all this time is to fix you some fresh coffee."

"All right." Then he'd get his tape recorder and his notebook and start doing what he'd come to do.

"The kitchen was a mess," she recalled. "Did you have any trouble finding breakfast?"

"Just coffee."

She bent over to pick up her bucket. Her back ached, just a bit. "I guess I can give you some bacon and eggs. I can guarantee the eggs're fresh."

He glanced into the bucket and saw a mound of light brown eggs. "You have chickens?"

"Over there." She indicated the shed he'd seen her come out of earlier. "They're the boys' responsibility in the summer. I haven't the heart to make them trudge around before school, so—"

He slipped. The ice was rapidly turning to slush. Next to him, Abby reached out, then slid herself. Instinctively they grabbed for each other, teetered, then righted themselves. Her face was buried in his shoulder, and she began to giggle.

"You wouldn't laugh if you'd landed on your back and broken your...eggs." His hand was deep in her hair. It shouldn't be, he knew, but it was so soft, and the neck beneath was so slender.

"I always laugh when I escape catastrophe." Still smiling, she looked up. Her face was flushed, her eyes glowing. Without thinking, without being able to think, he tightened the arm around her waist. The smile faded, but the glow in her eyes deepened. He was so close, his body so hard, and he was looking at her as though they'd known each other all their lives rather than one day.

She wished they had. She wished desperately that they had and that he was someone she could talk to, share with, lean on, just a little. His fingers brushed the nape of her neck and she shivered, though they were warm.

"I should have warned you—" she began. Suddenly she found her heart was beating too fast to allow her to think, much less speak.

"Warned me about what?" It was crazy. It was wrong. He had no business forgetting his purpose here in this sudden wild desire to taste her. But crazy or not, wrong or not, he wanted to feel her mouth meet his and give.

He lowered his head, watching her. The sun shone on her face, warm and bright, but her eyes were shadowed, and as wary as the mare's had been when he'd slipped the halter over her head.

"The path." Abby inched her head back in a gesture of confusion that was easily mistaken for teasing. Her eyes never left his. Her lips parted. "It gets slippery."

"So I found out." The fingers at the nape of her neck pressed lightly, drawing her closer, still closer, until their lips were only a whisper apart.

Longings, needs she'd thought she'd finished with, sprang out fresh and terribly strong. She wanted, oh, she wanted to give way to them and feel. Just feel. But she'd always been the sensible one. Only once had she forgotten that, and... She couldn't forget again. "Don't."

His mouth brushed over hers, and he felt the tremulous movement he knew women used as seduction. "I already have."

"No." She was weakening. The hand that she brought to his chest simply lay there. "Please don't."

Her breath was unsteady, her eyes half-closed. Dylan had little respect for a woman who pretended reluctance so that a man was left with the responsibility. And the blame. Need crawled through him, but he released her. His eyes were flat and cool as he nodded. "Your choice."

She was chilled and churning. There was something biting, something hurting, in his tone, but she couldn't think about that now. Careful of the melting ice, she picked her way back to the house.

After using the boot pull on the back porch, she took the eggs to the sink and began washing up. Dylan came in behind her. "If you'll give me a few minutes, I'll have something hot."

"Take your time." He walked past her and out of the kitchen.

She washed each egg meticulously, waiting for her mind to empty and her system to calm. Serenity was what she relied on, what she'd worked for. She couldn't allow an accidental embrace with a man she barely knew to change that. Hadn't he released her without a second's hesitation? Abby began to put the eggs in one of the empty cartons she kept under the sink. He was safe. She only sighed over that once.

She'd never been terribly sexual in any case, she reminded herself as she pulled a slab of bacon from the refrigerator. Hadn't Chuck pointed that out with complete clarity? She simply wasn't enough to fulfill a man's needs. Abby heated the cast-iron skillet and watched the bacon bubble and shrink. She was a good wife, dependable, responsible, sympathetic, but she wasn't someone a man burned for in the middle of the night.

She didn't need to be. She put on more water for coffee. She was happy being what she was. She intended to go on being what she was. Taking a deep breath, she unclenched her hands. Dylan was coming back.

"I didn't ask you how you wanted your eggs," she began then turned to see him set his tape recorder on the counter. Nerves threatened and were conquered. "You want to work in here?"

"Here's fine. And I'd like the eggs over easy." He found an uncluttered spot at the counter and sat. "Listen, Abby, I don't expect you to cook three meals a day for me."

"The check you sent for expenses was more than adequate." She broke an egg in the pan.

"I thought you'd have a staff."

"A staff of what?" She broke the second egg, then glanced over. Abruptly, nerves gone, she laughed. "A staff? As in maid and cook and so on?" Delighted, she shook her hair back, then gave the eggs her full attention. "Where in the world did you get an idea like that?"

Automatically he turned on the tape recorder. "Rockwell was wealthy, you were his heir. Most women in your position would have a servant or two."

She remained facing the stove so that her face was curtained by her hair. "I don't really care to have people around. I'm here most of the time; it'd be silly to have someone dusting around me."

"Didn't you have a staff before your husband died?"

"Not here. In Chicago." She scooped up his eggs. "That was before and right after Ben was born. We lived in a suite in his mother's house. She had a full staff. Chuck traveled a great deal, and we didn't really have a family yet, so we hadn't decided where to settle."

"His mother. She didn't approve of you."

Abby set the plate in front of him without a tremor. "Where did you hear that?"

"I heard all sorts of bits and pieces. It's part of the job. It couldn't have been easy living in Janice Rockwell's home when she didn't approve of the marriage."

"I don't think it's fair to say she didn't approve." Abby went back for coffee, choosing her words carefully. "She was devoted to Chuck. You probably knew she raised him alone when her husband died. Chuck was only seven then. It isn't easy raising children without a partner."

"You'd know about that."

She sent him an even look. "Yes, I would. In any case, Janice was very protective of Chuck. He was a dynamic, attractive man, the kind who attracted women. On the circuit, there are all manner of groupies hovering around."

"You weren't a fan."

"I never followed racing. We were always traveling around, playing in clubs and so forth. I didn't even know who Chuck was when we first met."

"Hard to believe."

She poured coffee into two cups on the counter. "Janice thought so, too."

"And resented you."

Abby took a calming sip of coffee. "Your job isn't to put words in my mouth, is it?"

She wasn't going to be easy to shake. It seemed to him that she had her answers down pat. Too pat. "No. Go on."

"Janice didn't resent me personally. She would have resented any woman who took Chuck away from her. It's only natural. In any case, I think we got along well enough."

Though he intended to dig a bit deeper there, he let it pass for now. "Why don't you tell me how you met Rockwell?"

That was easy. She could talk about that without hedging. "We were playing—my family and I—in a club in Miami. My parents did this little comedy routine and a couple of songs. Then my sisters and I ran through our bit—show tunes with a sprinkling of popular music. God, the costumes—" She broke off, laughing, then began to set the kitchen to rights as she talked. "Anyway, we did bring some business in. I always thought Chantel was responsible for that. She was stunning, and though she never had Maddy's range, she could sell a song. The race brought the drivers into town, the mechanics, backers, groupies. We always had a pretty good crowd."

He watched her move around the kitchen with a smile on her face as though she were amused by the memory. "Every night Pop had to ward men off who wanted to ah . . . see Chantel home. Then one night Chuck walked in with Brad Billinger."

"Billinger's retired now."

"He quit racing after Chuck was killed. They were close. Very close. I haven't seen him in a couple of years now, but he always sends the boys something on their birthdays and for Christmas. As soon as they sat down at a table, there was a lot of noise and confusion, right during the middle of a set. You get used to that kind of thing in clubs and have to know how to handle it. Noise, hecklers, drunks."

"I can imagine."

"Pop had delegated me to deal with that kind of problem when the three of us were on because Chantel tended to lose her temper and Maddy had a habit of walking right offstage until things calmed down again. So I leaned into the mike and made some joke, something about our next number being so dangerous that we needed absolute quiet. They didn't pay a lot of attention, but we kept on. Then we went into 'Somewhere,' from *West Side Story*. Do you know it?"

"I've heard it." Dylan leaned back and lit a cigarette. Eighteen, and handling drunks and hecklers. She couldn't be as soft as she looked.

"I looked over to where most of the noise was still coming from, and Chuck was looking right at me. It was an odd feeling. When you perform, people watch, but they rarely really look at you. At the break Chantel made a comment about Superdriver staring at me. That was the first inkling I had of what Chuck did for a living. Chantel was always reading gossip columns."

"Now she's in them."

"She loves every minute of it."

After searching through the kitchen drawers, Abby came up with the lid of a mason jar for Dylan to use as an ashtray. "Sorry, I don't have anything else."

"Chris has already given me your views on smoking. So it was love at first sight?"

"It was..." How did she explain? She'd been eighteen, and naive in ways the man sitting in her kitchen would never understand. "You could call it that. Chuck stayed until the last set was over, then came back and introduced himself. Maybe part of the attraction for him was that I really didn't know he was someone I should be impressed with. He was very polite and asked me to dinner. It was after midnight and he asked me to dinner."

She smiled again. She'd been so young and, like Chris, so gullible. "Of course, Pop wouldn't hear of it. The next afternoon there were two dozen roses delivered to the motel where we were staying. Pink roses. Nothing that romantic had ever happened to me. And that night he was back again. He kept coming back until he'd charmed my mother, persuaded my father and infatuated me. When he left Miami for the next race, I left with him. And I had his ring on my finger."

She glanced down. Now it was bare. "Life's a funny thing, isn't it?" she murmured. "You never know what trick it's going to pull next."

"How did your family feel about you marrying Chuck?"

She pulled herself back to the business at hand. Give him enough, Abby reminded herself. Just don't give him everything. "You'd have to understand that my family rarely all think the same thing about anything.

My mother cried, then altered her wedding dress to fit me even though we were married by a justice of the peace. Pop cried, too. After all, he was marrying me off to a stranger, and his act had just been shot to hell." Picking up an apple, she polished it absently on her sleeve. "Maddy said I was crazy, but that everyone deserved to do something crazy now and then. And Chantel..." She hesitated.

"Chantel what?"

It was time, she felt, for caution again. "Chantel's the oldest of the three of us—two and a half minutes older than me, but that still makes her big sister. She didn't think Chuck, or anyone, was good enough. She had plans to have a great many love affairs, and decided I was blowing my chance to have them, too." With a laugh, she bit into the apple. "If you believe everything you read, Chantel's had so many love affairs she's lucky to be alive. Trace didn't hear about the wedding until, oh, three or four months later. He sent me a crystal bird from Austria."

"Trace...that's your brother. Older brother. I don't have much information on him."

"Who does? I doubt it matters in this case, really. Trace never even met Chuck."

Dylan made a note anyway. "From there, you hit the circuit. Some might call it an odd sort of honeymoon."

In some ways, that entire first year had been a honeymoon. In other ways, there'd been no honeymoon at all, no solitary time for settling in and learning. "I'd traveled before." She shrugged. "I was born traveling, literally. Pop got my mother off a train in Duluth and to a hospital twenty minutes before she gave birth. Ten days later we hit the road again. Until this place, I'd never lived in one spot for more than six months at a time. You follow one circuit or you follow another.''

"But the Grand Prix's more exciting.''

"In some ways. But like performing, there's a lot of sweat and preparation for a few minutes in the spotlight.''

"Why did you marry him?''

She looked back at him. Her eyes were calm enough, but he thought her smile was just a little sad. "He was a knight on a white charger. I'd always believed in fairy tales.''

Chapter Four

She wasn't being honest with him. Dylan didn't need a lie detector to know that Abby veered away from the truth every time they talked. When she veered, she did so calmly, looking him straight in the eye. Only the slightest change in her tone, the briefest hesitation, tipped him off to the lie.

Dylan didn't mind lies. In fact, in his work he expected them. Reasons for them varied—self-preservation, embarrassment, a need to gloss over the image. People wanted to paint themselves in the best light, and it was up to him to find the shadows. A lie, or more precisely the reason for the lie, often told him more than a flat truth. His background as a reporter had taught him to base a story on fact, corroborated fact, then leave judgment to the reader. His opinion might leak through, but his feelings rarely did.

His main problem with Abby was that he'd yet to satisfy himself as to her motivation. Why lie, when the truth would undoubtedly sell more books? Sensationalism was more marketable than domestic bliss. She hadn't reached the point where she portrayed her marriage as idyllic, but she certainly had managed to skim over problem areas.

And there'd been plenty of them.

Alone in his room with only the desk lamp to shed light, Dylan took out a stack of tapes. A glance at this watch showed that it was just past midnight. The rest of the house was long since in bed, but then, regular hours had never been a part of his life. Schedules and time frames boxed a man in. Dylan didn't like walls unless he built them himself. He could work through the day if he chose, or he could work through the night, because hours didn't matter. Only the results.

The house was quiet around him, with only a faint wind scraping at the windows. He might have been alone—but he was aware, maybe too aware, that he wasn't. There were three people in the house, and he found them fascinating.

Chris and Ben, Dylan recalled sympathetically, had gone to their rooms after a firm scolding and a few tears. Using their mother's best china to feed the dog hadn't been the smartest move they could have made. She hadn't lifted a hand to them or even so much as shouted, but her lecture and disapproval had had both boys' chins dragging on the ground. A nice trick. Though it amused him, Dylan pushed the whole business aside. He had work to do, and a woman to figure out.

He'd already interviewed several people about Chuck Rockwell. Opinions and feelings about the man were varied, but none of them were middle-of-the-road. The one firm fact Dylan had picked up was that people had either adored Rockwell or detested him. Dylan picked up the tape marked Stanholz and turned it over in his hand.

Grover P. Stanholz had been Chuck's original backer, a wealthy Chicago lawyer with a love of racing and personal ties to the Rockwells. For ten years he'd played father, mentor and banker to Rockwell. He'd seen the young driver go from an eager rookie to one of the top competitors on the circuit. Just over a year before his death, Stanholz had pulled the financial rug out from under his famous protégé.

Thoughtful, Dylan slipped the tape into the recorder and ran it nearly to the end. It only took him a moment to find the spot he was looking for.

"Rockwell was a winner, a money-maker and a friend." Dylan's own voice came through the speaker, low and distinct. Automatically he turned the volume down so that the sound reached no farther then the end of his desk. "Why, when he was favored to win the French Grand Prix, did you pull out as his backer?"

There was a long silence, then a rustling sound. Dylan remembered that Stanholz had drawn out a cigar and taken his time unwrapping it. "As I explained, my interest in Chuck wasn't simply financial. I had been a close friend of his father's, was a friend of his mother's." There was another silence as Stanholz lit his cigar. "When Chuck started out, he was already a winner. You could see it in his eyes. The beauty was, he had a tremendous love and respect for the sport. He was . . . special."

"How?"

"He was going straight to the top. Whether I had backed him or he'd had to scramble to find the money to race, he was going to the top."

"Couldn't he have used the Rockwell money?"

"To race?" Stanholz's laugh came as a wheeze over the tape. "Chuck's money was tied up tight in trust. Janice adored that boy. She'd have never released the money so he could drive at 150 miles an hour. Believe me, she fried me for doing it, but the boy was hard to resist." It came on a sigh, wistful, regretful. "Men like Chuck don't come along every day. Racing takes a certain arrogance and a certain humility. It takes common sense and a disregard for life and limb. It's a balance. He was devoted to his profession and eager to make a name for himself. I've always wondered if the trouble was that he won too much too soon. Chuck began to see himself as indestructible. And unaccountable."

"Unaccountable?"

There was another pause here, a hesitation, then a quiet sigh. "Whatever he did, however he did it, was all right, because of who he was. He forgot, if you can understand what I mean, that he was human. Chuck Rockwell was on a collision course with himself. If he hadn't crashed in Detroit, he'd have done so elsewhere. I felt pulling out as his backer might give him something to think about."

"What do you mean, he was on a collision course with himself?"

"Chuck was racing his own engine. Sooner or later he was going to burn out."

"Drugs?"

"I can't comment on that." It was a lawyer's voice, dry and flat.

"Mr. Stanholz, it's been rumored that Rockwell had been using drugs, most specifically cocaine, for some time before his fatal crash in Detroit."

"If you want that substantiated, you'll have to go elsewhere. Chuck didn't die an admirable man, but he'd had his moments. I remember them."

Unsatisfied, Dylan stopped the recorder. It was a non-denial at best. He had substantiated through others who'd refused to go on record that Chuck Rockwell had developed a dangerous dependence on drugs. But he'd been clean during the last race. The autopsy had determined that. In any case, that was only one area. There were others.

The next tape was marked Brewer. Lori Brewer was the sister of the man who had been Rockwell's backer during his last year. The divorced former model was by her own admission a woman who liked men who took risks. Rockwell's wife hadn't been in the stands during his final race. But his mistress had.

Dylan put in the tape and pushed the play button.

"...the most exciting, dynamic man I've ever known."

Lori's voice had the low-key sensuality of the South. "Chuck Rockwell was a star, fast and hot. He knew his own worth. I admire that in a man."

"Ms. Brewer, for nearly a year you'd been Rockwell's constant companion."

"Lover," she corrected. "I'm not ashamed of it. Chuck was as devastating a lover as he was a driver. He did nothing by half measures." She gave a low, warm-sugar laugh. "Neither do I."

"Did it bother you that he was married?"

"No. I was there, she wasn't. Look, what kind of a marriage is it when people only see each other three or four times a year?"

"Legal."

He remembered she'd taken that good-naturedly enough, her only response a shrug. "Chuck was planning to divorce her anyway. The problem was that she had a stranglehold on his bank account. The lawyers were negotiating a settlement."

Dylan turned off the tape with a muttered oath. Not once during any of his conversations with Abby had she mentioned divorce. There was always the possibility that Rockwell had lied to Lori Brewer. But then, Dylan didn't believe the very sharp Ms. Brewer would have been duped for long. If divorce proceedings had been underway, Abby was doing her best to cover it.

Dylan hadn't pushed the point yet, nor had he brought up Lori Brewer. He was aware that once he did she would probably look at him as the enemy. Whatever he got out of her after that point would have to be pried out. So he'd wait. What he wanted from Abby had to be won through patience.

He pushed aside tapes of other drivers, mechanics, other women, and chose the one marked Abby. It didn't occur to him that out of all the tapes he had, hers was the only one not marked with just a last name. He'd stopped thinking of her as Mrs. Rockwell. The tape was from this morning, when he'd cornered her in the living room. She'd been folding laundry, and it had occurred to him that he hadn't seen anyone do that quiet, time-consuming little chore in more years than he could count. There'd been an old fifties record on the stereo, and the doo-wops and the sha-la-las had poured out as she'd sorted socks.

He remembered how she'd looked. Her hair had been pulled back in a ponytail so that her cheekbones stood out with subtle elegance. The collar of a flannel shirt had poked out of the neck of an oversize sweatshirt, leaving the curve and line of her body a mystery. She'd worn thick socks and no shoes. The fire had been crackling behind her, flames curling greedily around fresh logs. She'd looked so content and at peace with herself that for a moment he hadn't wanted to disturb her. But he'd had a job to do. Just as he had one to do now. Dylan pushed the play button again.

"Did racing put a strain on your marriage?"

"You should remember, Chuck was a driver when I married him." Her voice on the tape sounded calm and solid after Lori Brewer's honey-laced one. "Racing was part of my marriage."

"Then you enjoyed watching him race?"

There had been a lengthy pause as she'd given herself time to find the right words. "In some ways I think Chuck was at his best behind the wheel, on the track. He was exciting, almost eerily competent. Confident," she added, looking beyond Dylan into her own past. "So confident in himself, in his abilities, that it never occurred to me he would lose the race, much less lose control."

"But after the first eight or nine months you stopped traveling with your husband."

"I was pregnant with Ben." She'd smiled a little as she'd pulled a small, worn sweater out of the basket. "It became difficult for me to jump from city to city, race to race. Chuck was—" And there it was, Dylan noted, that slight variance in tone. "He was very understanding. It wasn't too long after that that we bought this place. A home base. Chuck and I agreed that Ben, then Chris, needed this kind of stability.''

"It's hard to picture a man with Chuck Rockwell's image settling down in a place like this. But then, he didn't settle, did he?''

She had very carefully folded a bright red sweatshirt. "Chuck needed a home port, like anyone else. But he also needed to race. We combined the two.''

Evasions, Dylan thought as he stopped the tape. Half-truths and outright lies. What game was she playing? And why? He knew her well enough now to be certain she wasn't stupid. She would have known of her husband's infidelities, and most particularly of his relationship with Lori Brewer. Protecting him? It hardly seemed feasible that she would protect a man who'd cheated on her, and one who'd cheated blatantly, in public, without a semblance of discretion.

Was she, had she been, the kind of woman content to stay in the background and keep the home fires burning? Or was she, had she been, a woman with her eye on the main chance?

And what kind of man had Rockwell been? Had he been the egotistical driver, the generous lover or the understanding husband and father? Dylan found it hard to believe any man could be all three. Abby was the only one who could give him the answers he needed.

Dragging a hand through his hair, he pushed away from the desk. He wanted to get something down on paper. Once he did, he might begin to put it all in some sort of perspective. Dylan looked at his typewriter and the tapes. Coffee, he decided. It was going to be a long night.

There was a low light burning in the hall. Automatically he glanced across the corridor to where Abby slept.

Her door was partially open, and the room was dark. He had an urge to cross over and push the door open a little wider so he could see her in the light from the hall.

What did he care for her privacy? He poked and scraped at her privacy whenever he questioned her. She'd cashed a check that gave him permission to.

No, he didn't give a damn for her privacy. But his own self-preservation was a different matter. If he looked, he'd want to touch. If he touched, he might not be able to pull back. So he turned from her room and started down the stairs, alone.

The fire in the living room was burning low and well. He'd watched Abby bank it one night and had been forced to admit that she did a better job of it than he would have. He left it alone and walked down the hall to the kitchen.

She was sitting at the bar in the dark. The only light came from the kitchen fire and the half-moon outside. She had her elbows on either side of a cup, her chin propped by both hands. He thought she looked unbearably lonely.

"Abby?"

She jumped. It might have been funny if he hadn't seen just how white her face was before she focused on him.

"Sorry, I didn't mean to scare you."

"I didn't hear you come down. Is anything wrong?"

"I wanted coffee." But instead of going to the stove, he went to her. "I thought you were in bed."

"Couldn't sleep." She smiled a little and didn't, as he'd expected, fuss with her hair or the lapels of her robe. "The water's probably still hot. I just made tea."

He slid onto the stool beside her. "Problem?"

"Guilt."

His reporter's instincts hummed, at war with an unexpected desire to put his arm around her and offer comfort. "About what?"

"I keep seeing the tears welling up in Chris's eyes when I sent him to bed without letting him watch his favorite show."

He didn't know whether to laugh at himself or her. "Odds are he'll recover."

"The plate wasn't that important." She lifted her tea, then set it down without drinking. "I never use them. They're ugly."

"Uh-huh. Maybe they should take a place setting or two out to the barn for the horses."

She opened her mouth, then laughed. This time, when she picked up her tea, she drank. It soothed a throat that was dry and a little achy. "I wouldn't go quite that far. Janice gave them to Chuck. To Chuck and me," she corrected, a little too quickly. "They're Wedgwood."

"And should be treated with due respect," he said. He hadn't missed her slip. "So what's the problem?"

"I hate to lose my temper."

"Did you? You never raised your voice."

"You don't have to yell to lose your temper." She looked out the window again and wished fleetingly that it wasn't so cold. If it were spring she could go out, sit on the porch and watch the sky. "It was only a plate, after all."

"And it was only a television show."

With a sigh, she settled against the back of the stool. "You think I'm being foolish."

"I suppose you're being a mother. I don't have much experience there."

"It's just so hard when you're the only one to make the rules and the decisions...and the mistakes." She combed a hand through her hair in an unconscious gesture that had it settling beautifully around her face. "Sometimes, late at night like this, I worry that I'm too hard on them. That I expect too much from them. They're just little boys. Now I've sent them off to bed, Chris sniffling and Ben sulking, and—"

Dylan interrupted her. "Maybe you're too hard on their mother." She stopped, stared at him, then looked at her tea again.

"I'm responsible."

And that was that, he could hear it in her tone. He started to drop it, to leave her to her own unhappiness. But whatever he thought of her, whatever he didn't think of her, he knew she was devoted to her children. "Look, I don't know a lot about kids, but I'd say those two are pretty normal and well adjusted. Maybe you should congratulate yourself instead of dragging out the sackcloth."

"I'm not doing that."

"Sure you are. You'll have the ashes out any minute."

She waited for the annoyance to come, but it didn't. Instead, she felt the guilt fade. "Thanks." At ease now, Abby warmed her hands on her cup. "I guess it helps to have a little moral support from time to time."

"No problem. I hate to see a woman sulking in her tea."

She laughed, but he couldn't be sure if it was at herself or at him. "I never sulk, but I'm a real champ at guilt. There were times when Ben was going through his terrible twos when I'd call my mother just to hear her tell me he probably wasn't going to be a homicidal maniac.''

"I'd have thought you'd talk to your husband about it.''

"That wouldn't have done any—" She cut herself off. It was late, and she was tired and much too vulnerable. "I'll make you that coffee," she began, and started to stand.

"I don't want you to wait on me." He had his hand on her arm, and though the touch was still light, it was enough to keep her from moving away.

She felt, incredibly, impossibly, an urge to just turn into his arms. She wanted to be held in them, to have him fold her to him and ask no questions. But of course he would. He would always ask, and she couldn't always answer. Abby held her ground and kept her distance.

"And I don't want you to interview me now.''

"You've never mentioned Chuck in the area of fatherhood, Abby. Why is that?''

"Maybe because you've never asked me.''

"So I'm asking now.''

"I told you, I'm not in the mood for an interview. It's late. I'm tired.''

"And you lie.'' His grip tightened just enough to make her heartbeat unsteady.

"I don't know what you're talking about.''

He was sick of evasions, sick of looking at her face and knowing the truth wouldn't be there. "Every time I touch on certain areas you give me these tidy answers. Very pretty and well rehearsed. I have to ask myself why. Why do you want to whitewash Chuck Rockwell?''

He was hurting her. Not her arm—she could barely feel his fingers on her—he was hurting her deep in places she'd deluded herself into believing were safe. "He was my husband. Isn't that answer enough for you?"

"No." He could hear the emotion trembling in her voice. So he'd push, and he'd push now. "The theory I've come up with is, the better he looked, the better you looked. And if your marriage seemed to be going well, Janice Rockwell was happy. Chuck was her only son, and somebody was bound to inherit all that money."

For the second time he watched her face pale, but this time he recognized rage, not fear. It ripped through her; he could feel it just by the touch of his hand on her arm. He wanted it. He wanted to tear holes in her composure and get to the truth. And to her.

"Let go of me." Her voice vibrated in the quiet kitchen. Behind them, a log broke and tossed sparks against the screen. Neither of them noticed.

"I want an answer first."

"You seem to have them already."

"If you want me to believe otherwise, tell me."

"I don't give a damn what you think." And that, Abby realized was the biggest lie of all. She cared, and because she cared, his accusation had crushed her. She'd been crushed before and understood that whining about it brought nothing but humiliation. "I'll give you what you want to hear and be done with it. I chose to exploit my marriage, to cash in on my dead husband's fame and reputation. Since I'm all but certain Janice Rockwell will read the book, I want to be sure she's satisfied with the results. Obviously I want her to see that my marriage to Chuck was solid. Whatever dirt you manage to dig up won't come from me. Satisfied?"

He let her arm go. In the space of seconds, she'd confirmed everything he'd thought of her, and contradicted everything he'd begun to feel. "Yeah, I'm satisfied."

"Fine. If you have more questions, ask them tomorrow, when the tape's running."

He watched her walk away and wondered how long it would take him to separate the lies from the truth.

Abby invariably woke quickly, and after her first half cup of coffee was completely alert and ready to take charge. Today, she found herself reluctant to leave her bed. Her muscles ached, her temples throbbed. Blaming it on a restless night, she went into her morning routine in low gear.

The boys were cheerful enough as they gobbled down their breakfast. The altercation of the evening before was already forgotten, in the way children had of putting things behind them. After she'd seen them off to school she indulged in another cup of coffee, waiting for her system to catch up with her schedule.

Still dragging, she bundled herself in her coat and went outside. The sun was bright, the air already warming with the first promise of spring, but she shivered and wished she'd put on an extra sweater. Catching a cold, she decided as she rubbed at the ache in the back of her neck. Well, she just didn't have time for it. Moving on automatic pilot, she gathered the eggs, then walked to the barn.

The stalls needed cleaning, the horses needed to be fed and groomed. For the first time in as long as she could remember, she resented the hours she spent working. All she ever did was clean up after others, take care of problems and deal with the jobs that had to be done. When was she going to have time for herself? Time to curl up with a book and while away an afternoon.

A book. Nearly laughing at herself, she gathered halters. Now wasn't the time to think of books—especially not one book in particular. She'd forgotten she could be hurt. It had been so long since she'd been involved with anyone who could—

Pressing her fingers against her eyes, Abby cut herself off. She couldn't call her relationship with Dylan an involvement. Business and business only, the kind that was meant to benefit both of them—that was all there was. It didn't matter, couldn't matter to her that he thought she was an opportunist. Abby supposed that was the kindest word for what he thought of her. If she followed her wounded feelings and tossed him out, she'd have accomplished nothing. In any case, she'd signed the papers and was committed to keeping him around.

And when did her obligations end? Abby let the first two horses loose in the paddock, then made the return trip to the barn. She'd been obligated to Chuck, then to her children. Now, because of them she was again duty-bound, however obliquely, to Chuck. So let Dylan Crosby think what he wanted of her as long as he wrote the book.

Tired, she rested her head against the gelding's flank. His flesh felt cool and friendly. God, she needed a friend. How could she think straight when her head was pounding? Yet she had to. The flare of temper last night might have cost her. If Dylan thought the worst of her, wouldn't it color his writing? Damn, what did he care about her reasons for authorizing the book? Whatever they were, he was being paid to write it. Her motivations had nothing to do with the story of Chuck's life. Yet they had everything to do with it.

She made a second trip outside and returned for the rest of the horses. After she'd finished in the barn, maybe her head would be clear. Then she'd know the right way to handle Dylan.

She remembered the morning when the sun had been bright and hard on her face and he'd held her. Wanted her. She could still remember the way his eyes had looked, the way his mouth had felt when it had brushed against hers. For a moment, for one indulgent moment, she'd wished he could be someone she could depend on, someone she could confide in. That was foolish. She'd known before they'd met that he had a job to do. So did she.

By the time she'd finished with the first stall, her skin was filmed with sweat. The pitchfork seemed heavier than usual as she lifted it to start on the next.

"Seems to me you ought to hire yourself a couple of hands."

Dylan stood just inside the door, the sun at his back, his face in shadow. Abby stopped long enough to squint at him. "Does it? I'll take it under advisement."

He picked up a pitchfork but just leaned on it. "Abby, why don't you drop this masquerade—you know, the struggling little homemaker who works from dawn to dusk to keep her family going."

She leaned into her work. "I'm trying to impress you."

"Don't bother. The book's about Chuck Rockwell, not you."

"Fine. I'll drop the act as soon as I get rid of this manure."

So she had claws. His fingers tightened on the worn wood handle until he deliberately relaxed them. He wanted to get to her, but he had to keep control to do it. "Listen, as long as things don't jibe, the book goes nowhere. Since we both want it to move, let's stop playing games."

"Okay." Because she needed to rest a moment, she stopped and leaned on her pitchfork. "What do you want, Dylan?"

"The truth, or as close as you can get to it. You were married to Rockwell for four years. That means there are parts of his life you know better than anyone. Those are the parts I want from you. Those are the parts you were paid to give me."

"I said I'd talk to you when the tape was running, and I will." She turned back to the stall. "Right now I've got work to do."

"Just drop it." Dylan grabbed her by the lapels and spun her around. Her pitchfork went clattering to the concrete. "Call back whoever usually takes care of this business and let's get to work. I'm tired of wasting time."

"My staff?" She'd have pulled away, but she didn't think she had the strength. "Sorry, I gave them the month off. If you want to work, bring your little pad and tapes out here. My horses need tending."

"Just who the hell are you?" he demanded, giving her a quick shake. He was no less surprised than she when her knees buckled. Keeping his grip firm, he braced her against the stall. "What's the matter with you?"

"Nothing." She tried to brush his hands away but failed. "I'm not used to being knocked around."

"You get jostled more on the subway," he muttered. She made him feel like a rough-handed clod, and he hated it. He let her go.

"You'd know more about that than I." Infuriated with herself, she bent down to scoop up the pitchfork. When her head spun, she grabbed the side of the stall for support.

Swearing, Dylan took her by the shoulders. "Look, if you're sick—"

"I'm not. I'm never sick, I'm just a little tired."

And pale, he realized as he let himself really look at her. He yanked off his glove and held a hand to her face. "You're burning up."

"I'm just overheated." Her voice rose a bit with her panic at being touched, even though being touched was exactly what she needed. "Leave me alone until I'm finished in here."

"Can't stand a martyr," he mumbled, taking her by the arm.

It was rare, very rare, for Abby's Irish heritage to break through in sheer blind rage. She'd always left that to the rest of her family and calmly worked her way through difficulties. This wasn't one of those times. She yanked her arm away and shoved him hard against the side of the stall. The strength she'd dredged up surprised them both.

"I don't care what you can stand. I don't give a damn what you think. Those papers I signed don't give you the right to interfere in my life. I'll let you know when I have time for your questions and for your accusations. Whether you believe it's a game or a facade, I have work to do. You can go to hell."

She was panting as she turned and grasped the handles of the wheelbarrow. She jerked it up, took two steps, then dropped it again as her strength drained away.

"You're doing great." He was fed up with her, and with himself, but he'd have to deal with that later. Now, unless he was very much mistaken, the lady needed a bed. This time, when he took her by the arm, she could do no more than try to shake him off.

"Don't put your hands on me."

"Babe, I've been doing my damnedest to keep them off you all week." When she stumbled, he swore, then scooped her up in his arms. "This time we're both going to have to put up with it."

"I don't have to be carried." Then she started to shiver. Too weak to help herself, she let her head fall on his shoulder. "I haven't finished."

"Yeah, you have."

"The eggs."

"I'll get them later—after I dump you in bed."

"Bed?" She roused herself again, noticing dimly they were stepping onto the porch. "I can't go to bed. The horses haven't been dealt with, and the vet's coming at one to look over the mares. Mr. Jorgensen's coming with him. I have to sell that foal."

"I'm sure Jorgensen's going to be thrilled to buy the foal after you've given him the flu."

"Flu? I don't have the flu, just a little cold."

"Flu." Dylan laid her on the bed, then began to pry off her boots. "I'd say you'll be hobbling around again in a couple of days."

"Don't be absurd." She managed with a great deal of effort to prop herself up on her elbows. "I just need a couple of aspirin."

⌐ "Can you get undressed by yourself, or do you want help?"

"I'm not getting undressed," she said evenly, though if she could have had one wish at the moment, it would have been to sleep.

"Help then." Sitting down, he began to unbutton her coat.

"I don't need or want your help." She clung to what dignity she had left and struggled to sit up. "Look, I might have a touch of the flu, but I also have two children who'll walk in the door at 3:25. In the meantime I have to groom the horses, Eve in particular. I have a lot riding on the deal with Jorgensen."

Dylan studied her face. Her skin was pale, her eyes glazed with fever. The quickest way to bring her around was to agree with her. "Okay, that's at one. Do yourself a favor and rest for an hour." When she started to object, he shook his head. "Abby, you'll really impress Jorgensen by fainting at his feet."

She was wobbly. There was no use denying it. To be honest, she didn't think she could have lifted a curry comb at the moment. She was a practical woman, and the practical thing to do was to rest until she built up a little strength. If it galled a bit to agree with him, she'd just have to swallow the gall. "I'll rest an hour."

"Fine, get into bed. I'll bring you a couple aspirin."

"Thanks." She peeled off her coat as he rose. Then, as it had a habit of doing, her conscience poked at her. "Really. I appreciate it."

"No problem."

When he left, Abby took a grip on the bedpost and pulled herself out of bed. Her body punished her by throbbing all over. Moving slowly, she went to her dresser and pulled out a cotton gown. She tugged off her sweater, then her jeans. Exhausted from the effort, she stood rocking on her feet and shivering. Just an hour, she told herself, and I'll be fine.

Later, she couldn't even remember dragging on the gown and crawling into bed.

Dylan found her there when he came back. Sprawled on her stomach, she was sleeping, so deeply that she never stirred when he tucked the blankets around her. Nor did she stir when he bent closer and brushed the hair away from her face.

She never stirred for the hour he sat in the chair beside the bed, watching her. And wondering.

Chapter Five

Sweaty, aching and disoriented, Abby woke. How long had she been asleep? Pressing the heels of her hands against her eyes, she tried to gather her reserves of strength. Her skin felt clammy, and she thought for a moment that the lining of her throat had been coated with something hot and bitter. She was forced to admit that whatever had hit her had hit her with both fists. Because she was alone, she moaned a little as she sat up. Then, studying the clock beside her, she moaned again.

2:15. She'd slept nearly four hours. Mr. Jorgensen. Desperate, Abby swung out of bed. The pounding in her head began immediately, along with a throbbing that seemed to reach every inch of her body. She realized she was damp with sweat. Abby snatched up her jeans, then leaned against the bedpost, waiting for the weakness to pass.

They might still be here, she told herself. They could have come late and right now be standing in the barn, looking over the mare. Eve hadn't been groomed, but Jorgensen had already seen her at her best. And the vet—the vet was bound to vouch for the fact that the mare was strong and healthy. All she had to do was get dressed and go outside and apologize.

Dylan strolled in, carrying a tray. "Going somewhere?"

"It's after two." Though weak, it was definitely an accusation.

"You got that right." He set the tray down on the dresser and studied her. The nightgown scooped low at her neck and drooped carelessly over one shoulder—one very slender, very smooth shoulder. The rest of her was just as slender, from the long dancer's legs to the high, subtly rounded breasts.

A man was entitled, Dylan told himself, to feel a little tightening, a little heat, a little longing, when he looked at a half-naked woman and a rumpled bed. He just couldn't let it get personal. "Interesting," he murmured. "This is the first time I've seen you in something that isn't three inches thick."

"I'm sure I look ravishing."

"Actually, you look like hell. Why don't you get back in bed before you keel over?"

"Mr. Jorgensen—"

"An interesting little man," Dylan finished. Walking to her, Dylan took the jeans out of her hand and tossed them on a chair. "He talked about his horses with more passion than he did his wife." He eased her down on the bed as he spoke.

"He's still here? I've got to go out and talk to him."

"He's gone." With little fuss, Dylan arranged the pillows at her back.

"Gone?"

"Yeah. Open up. I managed to find this among the bottles of antiseptic spray and colored Band-Aids."

She waved the thermometer away as she tried to concentrate on her next move. "I can call him and reschedule. Did you explain why I wasn't available? I can't believe I missed him. The vet . . . did the vet . . . ?"

Dylan stuck the thermometer in her mouth, then captured both her hands before she could pull it out again. "Shut up." When she started to mumble around it, he caught her chin in his other hand. "Listen, if you want to hear about Jorgensen you'll leave that thing in and keep your mouth shut. Got it?"

She slumped back, nearly ready to sulk. He was speaking to her as she might to one of the boys. Seeing no alternative, Abby nodded.

"Good." Releasing her hands, he went back for the tray.

Abby immediately pulled the thermometer out. "Did the vet give Eve an exam? I need to—"

"Put that thing back in or I'll leave you up here alone and wondering." After setting the tray on her lap, he stood waiting. He felt a nice sense of satisfaction when she obeyed. "The vet said Eve was in perfect shape, that he didn't foresee any complications, and you can expect her to deliver the foal within a week."

She reached for the thermometer. He only had to lift a brow to stop her. "About the other mare, Gladys?" When she nodded, he shook his head. "Hell of a name for a horse. Anyway, she's just as fit. Jorgensen said to tell you if all goes well he'll call you to discuss terms after the foal's born. He also said," Dylan continued, grabbing her wrist again as she reached up, "that he has a couple of names for you. People who might be interested in the other foal. I have a feeling he might be interested himself if his wife doesn't skin him. You can call him when you're on your feet. Satisfied?"

She closed her eyes and nodded. It was happening, at last it was really happening. The money from the foals would go a long way toward paying off the rest of the loan she'd been forced to take after Chuck's death. To be nearly out of debt, to know that in a year or two she'd be essentially stable again. Foolishly she wanted to cry. She wanted to burrow under the covers and weep until tears of relief washed everything else away. Keeping her eyes closed, she waited until she could compose herself.

An odd woman, Dylan thought as he watched her. Why should she get so emotional over the sale of a couple of horses? He was certain the price was right, but it could hardly be more than a drop in the bucket compared to the estate she must have inherited from Rockwell. Money must be important, he decided, though he'd be damned if he could see where she spent it.

The furniture perhaps. Her bed was eighteenth-century and not something you'd pick up at a yard sale. And the horses, of course. She hadn't bought that stallion for a song and a smile. He glanced over at her closet. He'd wager that a good chunk of the rest was hanging in there.

When she opened her eyes again, he plucked the thermometer out. "Dylan I don't know what to say."

"Um-hmm. A hundred and three. Looks like you win the prize."

"A hundred and three?" Her gratitude disappeared. "That's ridiculous, let me see it."

He held it out of reach. "Are you always such a lousy patient?"

"I'm never sick. You must have read that wrong."

He handed it over, then watched as her brows drew together. "Well, that should make you feel a whole lot worse." He took the thermometer again, shook it, then slipped it into its plastic case. "Now, can you feed yourself or do you want help?"

"I can manage." She stared without appetite at the soup steaming on the tray. "I don't usually eat lunch."

"Today you do. We're pushing fluids. Try the juice first."

She took the glass he handed her, then sighed. No wonder he was treating her like one of the boys, she thought. She was acting like one. "Thanks. I'm sorry for complaining. I don't mean to be cranky, but there are so many things I have to do. Lying here isn't getting them done."

"Indispensable, are you?"

She looked at him again. Something moved in her eyes—emotion, hope, questions, he couldn't tell which. "I am needed."

She said it with such quiet desperation that he reached out to stroke her cheek before he thought about it. "Then you'd better take care of yourself."

"Yeah." She lifted the spoon and tried to work up some enthusiasm for the soup. "I *am* a lousy patient. Sorry."

"It's all right. So am I."

To please him, she began to eat. "You don't look like you're ever sick."

"If it makes you feel better, I had the flu a couple of years ago."

She smiled, a self-deprecating humor in her eyes. "It does. Anyway, I'm more used to doing the doctoring. Both boys were down with the chicken pox in September. The house was like a ward. Dylan..." She'd been working up to this for some time. Now, idly stirring her soup, she thought she had the courage. "I'm sorry about last night, and this morning."

"Sorry for what?"

She looked up. He seemed so relaxed, so untouched. Apparently harsh words and arguments didn't leave him churning with guilt. But he hadn't lied, and they both knew it. She figured they both knew she'd go on lying. "I said things I didn't mean. I always do when I'm angry."

"Maybe you're more honest when you're angry than you think." He was tense. However it looked on the outside, he was baffled by her, moved by her. "Listen, Abby, I still intend to push you and push you hard. But I've got some scruples. I don't intend to start wrestling with you until you can hold your own."

She had to smile. "As long as I'm sick, I'm safe."

"Something like that. You're not eating."

"I'm sorry." She set down the spoon. "I just can't."

He picked up the tray to set it beside the bed. "Anyone ever tell you that you apologize too much?"

"Yes." She smiled again. "Sorry."

"You're an interesting woman, Abby."

"Oh?" It felt so good just to snuggle back. Chilled, she drew the blankets higher. Incredibly, she was tired again, so tired it would have taken no effort at all to simply ease back and drift off. "I always thought I was rather humdrum."

"Humdrum." He glanced down at her elegant hands and remembered how competently they had worked. He remembered the woman in mink, diamonds glittering at her ears, and thought of how she had folded laundry. It didn't add up to humdrum. It simply didn't add up at all. "I've got a picture of you in my file that was taken in Monte Carlo. You were wrapped to the eyebrows in white mink."

"The white mink." She smiled drowsily as the energy drained from her degree by degree. "Made me feel like a princess. It was fabulous, wasn't it?"

"Was?"

"Mmm. Just like a princess."

"Where is it?"

"The roof," she said, and slept.

The roof? She had to be delirious if she was picturing fur coats on the roof. She murmured a bit when he settled her more comfortably.

A very interesting woman, Abby, he thought again as he stood back to look at her. All he had to do was fill in all the blank spaces.

When Dylan heard the first crash, he was in the middle of transcribing his notes on Rockwell's first year of professional racing. He swore, though without heat, as he turned off the typewriter. Leaving the half-typed sheet in the machine, he went downstairs to greet the boys at the front door.

"It wasn't my fault." Ben glared at his brother, his arm around the dog.

"It was, too, you—" Chris reached into his vocabulary and brought out his top insult "—Idiot."

"You're the idiot. Just because—"

"Problem?" Dylan asked as he opened the door. Both boys had fire in their eyes, and Chris was covered with mud from head to foot, as well. His bottom lip trembled as he pointed a dirty, self-righteous finger at his brother.

"He pushed me down."

"I did not."

"I'm telling Mom."

"Hold it, hold it." Dylan blocked the door and got a smear of fresh mud on his jeans. "Ben, don't you think you're a little too big to be pushing Chris down?"

"I didn't." His chin poked out. "He's always saying I did things when I didn't. *I'm* telling Mom."

Big tears welled up in Chris's eyes as he stood, a major mess, on the porch. Dylan had a strong and unexpected urge to hunker down and hug him. "Look, it'll clean off," he said, contenting himself with flicking at the boy's nose with a finger. "Why don't you tell me what happened?"

"He pushed me down." The first tears spilled over. He was still too young to be ashamed of them. "Just 'cause he's bigger."

"I did not." Not far from tears himself, Ben stared at the ground. "I didn't mean to, anyway. We were just fooling around."

"An accident?"

"Yeah." He sniffled, embarrassing himself.

"It never hurts to apologize for an accident." He put a hand on Ben's shoulder. "Especially when you're bigger."

"I'm sorry," he mumbled, shooting a look at his brother. "Mom's going to be mad 'cause he's got mud all over. I'm going to get in trouble. And it's Friday."

"Uh-huh." Dylan considered. Chris was over his tears now and running his fingers curiously through the mud on his coat. "Well, maybe we won't have to tell her this time."

"Yeah?" Hope sprang into Ben's eyes, then was quickly displaced by mistrust. "She's gonna see anyhow."

"No, she's not. Come on." Seeing no other way, Dylan hoisted Chris up. "We'll dump you in the washing machine."

He giggled and swung a friendly, filthy arm around Dylan's neck. "You can't put people in there. It's too small. Where's Mom?"

"Upstairs. She's got the flu."

"Like Mr. Petrie?"

"That's right."

Ben stopped as they entered the kitchen. "Mom's never sick."

"She is this time. Right now she's sleeping, so let's try to keep it down, okay?"

"I want to see her myself."

Dylan stopped in the act of pushing the door to the laundry room open. He glanced back and saw Ben just inside the kitchen, his mouth set, his eyes defiant. Though it disconcerted him, Dylan found himself admiring Ben's determination to defend his mother.

"Don't wake her up." He swung through to the laundry room. "Okay, tiger, strip."

Ready to oblige, Chris struggled out of his coat. "My teacher had the flu last week, so we had a substitute. She had red hair and couldn't remember our names. Is Mom going to be sick tomorrow?"

"She won't be as sick tomorrow." Dylan found the soap and began figuring out the mechanics of the washing machine.

"She can use my crayons." Chris plopped down on the floor and began yanking at his boots. "And we can read her stories. She reads me stories when I'm sick."

"I'm sure she'll appreciate it."

"If she feels real bad, I can let her have Mary."

"Who's Mary?"

"Mary's my dog, the one Aunt Maddy gave me when I was little. I still sleep with her, but don't tell Ben. He teases me."

Dylan smiled and sent water gushing into the machine. It was nice to be trusted. "I won't say anything."

"If she's better tomorrow, do you think we can go to the movies? She said she'd take us to the movies on Saturday."

"I don't know." Turning back, Dylan saw that the boy had taken him at his word. He'd stripped down to the skin. His sturdy little body was covered with goose bumps and dirt. "I don't think we have to go that far." After taking a folded towel off the dryer, Dylan bent down and wrapped the boy in it. "You're going to need a bath."

"I hate baths." Chris tilted his head and gave Dylan a solemn look. "I really hate them."

"Trouble is, you were right." Dylan dumped the rest of the clothes in the machine and closed the lid. "You won't fit in the washing machine."

Laughing, Chris raised his arms in an open, uncomplicated gesture that left Dylan speechless. Helpless to do anything but respond, Dylan lifted him up. Good God, he thought as he nuzzled him, I've managed to keep things in perspective for over thirty years and now I'm falling for a six-year-old kid with mud on his face.

"About that bath."

"Hate them."

"Come on, you're bound to have a boat or something to fool around with in there."

Resigned, Chris let himself be carried toward the inevitable. "I like trucks better."

"So take a truck."

"Can I take three?"

"As long as there's room for you." He set Chris down again by the bathroom door. "Now you've got to be quiet, right?"

"Right," Chris returned in a whisper. "Are you going to help me wash my hair? I can almost do it myself."

"Ah . . ." He thought about the work waiting on his desk. "Sure. Get yourself started."

Baby-sitting, Dylan thought as he hesitated in the hall, hadn't been part of the deal. Still, he knew Abby wasn't enjoying it any more than he was. He glanced at Ben's room. The door was closed. His first thought was to leave the boy to himself and deal with the less complicated task of washing Chris's hair. Swearing at himself, Dylan walked over and knocked.

"You can come in."

Dylan opened the door to see the boy sitting on his bed, an army of miniature men spread out in front of him. "Did you see your mother?"

"Yeah. I didn't wake her up." He sent two of the men crashing together. "I guess she's pretty sick."

"She just needs to rest for a couple of days." Dylan sat on the edge of the bed and picked up one of the men. "She'll probably want some company later."

"Once I came home from school and she was on the couch because she said she had this headache. But I knew she'd been crying."

At a loss, Dylan lined up men in tandem with Ben's. "Moms need to cry sometimes. Everybody does, really."

"Not guys."

"Yeah. Sometimes."

Ben digested that, but he wasn't ready to believe it. "Was Mom crying again?"

"This time she's just sick. I guess she'll feel better if we don't give her any trouble."

"I don't mean to cause trouble." Ben's voice was very young and very small.

"I'm sure you don't." Dylan thought of himself, of how he'd pushed and tugged and pressured. His job. But it didn't go very far toward the guilt.

"I didn't really mean to push Chris down in the mud," he mumbled.

"I didn't think you did." But Dylan *had* meant to push Abby up against a wall.

"Mom would've punished me."

"I see." Dylan found himself admiring Ben's candor, but now he'd have to do something, and what the hell did he know about handling kids? He dragged a hand through his hair and tried to be logical. "I guess we'll have to think of something. Want me to go push you down in the mud?"

Ben glanced up warily. After meeting Dylan's eyes, he laughed. "Then Mom would be mad at you."

"Right. Why don't you do Chris's chores tonight?"

"Okay." That was no big deal. He liked spending time with the horses, and Chris usually got in the way.

It both pleased and surprised Dylan that he could read the boy's mind. "That includes the dishes—it's Chris's turn."

"But—"

"It's a tough old world, kid." Dylan tugged his earlobe and went to see to his other charge.

* * *

Abby awoke to the sounds of an argument. An argument in whispers was still an argument. Opening her eyes, she focused on her sons, who were standing at the foot of the bed.

"We should wake her up now," Ben insisted.

"We should wait until Dylan comes up."

"Now."

"What if she still has a temperature?"

"We'll take it and find out."

"Do you know how?" Chris demanded, ready to be impressed.

"You use that little skinny thing. We just put it in her mouth, then wait."

"While she's asleep?"

"No, dummy. We have to wake her up."

"I'm awake." Abby pushed herself up against the pillows while both boys eyed her.

"Hi." Not at all sure how to deal with a sick mother, Ben fooled with the bedspread.

"Hi yourself."

"Are you still sick?"

Her throat was so dry that she was surprised she could talk at all. Every muscle in her body rebelled as she pushed herself up a bit higher. "Maybe a little."

"Do you want my crayons?" Not one to stand on ceremony, Chris crawled onto the bed to get a closer look.

"Maybe later," she told him, running a hand through his hair. "Did you just get home from school?"

"Heck, no. We've been home forever. Right, Ben?"

"We had dinner," Ben confirmed. "And did the chores."

"Dinner?" After she'd cleared her mind of sleep, she saw that the light was dim with evening. A glance at the clock had her moaning. She'd lost another three hours. "What did you have?"

"Tacos. Dylan makes them real good. Do you have a temperature?" Interested, Chris put his hand on her head. "You feel hot. Do you have to take medicine like Ben and me did? I can read you a story after."

"You can't read," Ben said in disgust.

"I can too. Miss Schaeffer said I read real good."

"Kid stuff, not Mom's kind of stories."

"Fighting again?" Dylan walked in with another tray. "It's nice to see everything's normal. Scoot over, Chris. Your mom has to eat."

"We all made it," Chris told her as she shifted aside. "Dylan made the eggs and Ben heated the soup. I made the toast."

"Looks great." She wished she could toss it, tray and all, out the window. When Dylan arranged the pillows behind her, she glanced up and saw the grin. Apparently writers read minds. Since he did, he'd also be aware that she had no choice but to eat.

"Dylan said you need your strength," Ben put in.

"Did he?"

"And Dylan said we had to be quiet so you could rest. We were real quiet." Chris waited for his mother to sample the toast he'd smeared overgenerously with butter.

"You were very quiet," Abby told him, washing down the soggy toast with juice.

"Dylan said he'd play a game with us later if we didn't mess up." Chris sent him a sunny smile. "We didn't, did we?"

"You did just fine."

Unwilling to let Chris get all the attention, Ben moved closer. "Dylan said you'd probably be too sick to go to the movies tomorrow."

"It seems Dylan says a lot," she murmured, then reached out to touch Ben's cheek. "We'll have to see. How was school?"

"It was pretty good. A bird got into the classroom during math and Mrs. Lieter chased it around. It kept crashing into the windows."

"Pretty exciting."

"Yeah, but then she opened one of the windows and got a broom."

"Tricia fell on the playground and got a big bump on her head." Chris leaned over to fuss with the thin gold chain his mother wore, which had fascinated him since childhood. "She cried for a long time. I fell down and didn't cry at all. Well, not very much," he corrected meticulously. "Dylan was going to put me in the washing machine."

Abby stopped running a hand over Chris's hair. "I beg your pardon?"

"Well, there was all this mud and stuff and—"

Dylan interrupted before Chris's storytelling got his brother in deep water. "A little accident, it's still pretty slippery outside."

As Abby looked on, Ben tilted his head and sent Dylan a quick sidelong look. A mixture of guilt and gratitude. "I see." At least she thought she did. She was also wise enough not to pursue it. "This is a great dinner, you guys, but I don't think I can eat any more right now."

Dylan took the remaining juice off the tray and set it on the nightstand. "Why don't you two take the tray down? I'll be along in a minute."

As soon as they'd gone, Dylan picked up the thermometer.

"Dylan, I really appreciate all this. I don't know what to say."

"Good." He stuck the thermometer in her mouth. "Then you can be quiet."

Unwilling to start another battle she'd lose, Abby sat back and waited until he drew the thermometer out again. "It's down, right?"

"Up two-tenths," he corrected, entirely too cheerfully for her taste, and handed her the aspirin.

"The boys were counting on that movie tomorrow."

"They'll survive." After replacing the thermometer, he started to leave her. Abby grabbed his hand impulsively.

"Dylan, I'm not trying to be a bad patient, but I swear I'll go crazy if I spend another minute alone in this bed."

He cocked his head. "Is that an invitation?"

"What? Oh, no." She snatched her hand back. "I didn't mean that. I only meant—"

"I get the picture." Bending over, he wrapped the spread around her and lifted her into his arms.

"What are you doing?"

"Getting you out of bed. I'll take you down, plop you in front of the TV. Odds are you'll be dead to the world inside of an hour."

"I've already slept all day." This time she could allow herself to enjoy, to appreciate, the sensation of being held in strong arms, of being carried as though she were fragile. For tonight, just for tonight, she could pretend there was someone to stand by her, to stand with her. Fairy tales, Abby warned herself, and stopped before she could lay her head on his shoulder.

"I appreciate you watching the children like this. I don't want to impose, though. I can call a neighbor."

"Forget it." He said it lightly, not wanting to admit he'd enjoyed the afternoon. "I can handle them. I worked my way through college as a bouncer."

"That kind of experience certainly helps," she murmured. "Dylan, did Chris get hurt when Ben pushed him down?"

"I don't know what you're talking about."

"You certainly do."

"Did Chris look hurt to you?"

"No, but—"

"Then you wouldn't want me to be a stool pigeon, would you?"

She sent him a mild look as he settled her down on the living room couch. "Men always stick together, don't they?"

Without answering, he switched on the set. He'd needed to set her down quickly, to break contact. She'd seemed so sweet, so small, so frail in his arms. A man made his biggest mistakes when he was sucked in by fragility.

"If you need anything, we'll be in the kitchen. Men stuff, you know?"

"Dylan—"

"Look, if you thank me again I'm going to belt you." Instead he bent down, took her face in his hands and kissed her, hard. "Don't thank me and don't apologize."

"I wouldn't dream of it." Before she could think, before she could reason, Abby reached out and brought his mouth back to hers again.

It wasn't sweet. It wasn't magic. It was solid and strong. She tasted, for the first time in too many years, the flavor of man. She wanted, for the first time in too many years. And wasn't it wonderful just to want again—not to think, not to reason, just to let go and want.

The touch, the taste, brought back no memories of her marriage, of the only other man she'd known. It was fresh and new, as beginnings should be.

Her skin was hot. He felt the yielding he knew came as much from weakness as from passion. Yet he thought, or rather wanted to think, that there was something more, something unique in the way her mouth fit his. So he wanted more. From the kiss alone, desire sprinted out until he wanted everything—to feel her skin, feverishly hot under the thin nightgown, to feel her body melt against his.

There was no artifice in her kiss, no expertise. The gesture seemed to be as pure and as generous as Chris lifting his arms to him. He drew away, reluctant and more than a little puzzled. He was finding that the more he knew her, the less he knew.

She lay back, her eyes half-closed, knowing he was studying her and helpless to slip on any mask. Whatever he wanted to see was there. She had no way of knowing that his own doubts were blinding him.

"That's something else we're going to deal with when you're on your feet, Abby."

"Yes, I know."

"You'd better rest." He put his hands in his pockets because it would be too easy to touch her again and forget.

"I will." She closed her eyes because it would be too easy to reach out again and forget. There were children in the next room. Her children, her responsibility. Her life.

When she opened her eyes again, he was gone.

Chapter Six

She didn't remember going back upstairs, but in the morning she woke in her own bed. And she woke late. There was something warm and fuzzy against her cheek. Her initial alarm turned to puzzlement, then to love, as she cuddled the ragged stuffed dog Chris prized. He must have brought it to her as she'd slept. Shifting, she saw the big pink sheet of contact paper taped sloppily to the bedpost that read Get Well Mom.

She recognized Ben's slanted, uneven printing, and tears blurred her vision. Maybe they were monsters, but they were her monsters, and they came through when it counted.

Did she? She rubbed Mary absently against her cheek. It was nearly ten in the morning, and she hadn't even fixed her children breakfast.

Disgusted, Abby pulled herself out of bed. Pretending her legs didn't wobble, she yanked her robe out of the closet and headed for the shower. There were things to be done, and she couldn't accomplish them in bed.

After she'd cleared the tub of a convoy of trucks, she just stood under the spray. It beat against aching muscles and feverish skin. She braced her hands against the tile and lifted her face so that the water sluiced over her. Gradually the chill passed and her mind cleared.

Dylan. Was it wrong that when her mind cleared he was the first thing to form in it? Perhaps it wasn't wrong, but it certainly wasn't safe. She'd started more there than she'd bargained for. Alone, she could admit that she hadn't the vaguest idea what to do next. The attraction she felt for him hadn't been in the plans. The wisest move would be to ignore it. But could she? Would he?

Once before, she'd felt this kind of quick excitement. And once before, she'd acted without giving herself a chance to reason. It wasn't a mistake she could afford to make twice. She couldn't say how long it had taken her to get over the hurt Chuck had caused, but she knew she couldn't deal with that sort of pain again. No, she didn't think she would survive to rebuild a second time, so the choice was clear. No involvement was worth the risk of losing. No man was worth the price. Now she had children to think of, a home, and the life she'd made for them.

Overlaying the doubts she had about herself were doubts about the project that had brought Dylan to her. It was going to be more difficult to evade, to lie, to hide, if she let herself feel something for him. So she couldn't.

Abby wearily turned off the shower. She couldn't risk feeling or giving or even taking when it came to Dylan.

She'd stick by her plan because the plan was survival; he was only the biographer of her children's father.

Dry, she walked back into the hall. A quick peek showed her the boys were already up. She'd go down, fix coffee, make them breakfast and get them away from their cartoons long enough to feed the stock.

She found them where she'd expected, huddled in front of the TV with the latest action-adventure cartoon whizzing by on the screen. What she hadn't expected was to find Dylan huddled with them.

"You call this a cartoon?" Chris was snuggled beside him on the sofa and Ben lay sprawled at his feet as though the three of them spent every Saturday morning together.

"It's a great cartoon," Ben told him. "Asteroid John tracks down the bad guys, but he never gets them all. Especially Dr. Disaster."

Dylan thought he knew who Ben was rooting for. "Listen, Bugs Bunny's a cartoon. It has style and wit, not just laser beams. Wile E. Coyote trying to catch the Roadrunner. Bugs outmaneuvering Elmer Fudd. That's a cartoon."

Ben just snorted and gave Asteroid John his attention.

Chris tugged on Dylan's shirt. "I like Bugs Bunny." Amused by the boy's earnest face, Dylan swung an arm over his shoulders.

"Chris looks like Bugs Bunny," Ben stated. He grinned, waiting for retaliation. Before Chris could scramble down, Dylan shifted the boy onto his lap.

"Nope," he said after a careful study of Chris's face. "Ears are too short. But Ben..." Reaching down, he tugged on an unguarded ear. "These might just make it."

Giggling, Ben put both hands over his ears and rolled over. "I'm Dr. Disaster and I'm going to blow up the planet Kratox."

"Yeah? You and who else?" He scooped the boy up and held him in a loose headlock. "You space marauders are all the same."

"Evil?"

"No, ticklish." He dug a finger into the boy's ribs and sent him squealing. It only took a moment for the three of them to roll off the sofa. Delighted, Chris climbed onto Dylan's shoulders. It was then he saw his mother standing in the doorway.

"Hi, Mom."

"Good morning." She watched her sons, who were flushed from the tussle, then looked at Dylan. He hadn't shaved, and might have been any man on a lazy Saturday morning.

"We're not supposed to roughhouse on the furniture," Ben whispered in Dylan's ear.

"Right." Dylan untangled himself, then gave Abby a long, measuring look. "You should be in bed."

"I'm fine, thanks." Why did he become only more arousing when he was a little rough around the edges? Would she always be attracted to men who had so little tenderness in them? "I'm just going to fix some coffee."

"It's on the stove."

"Oh." She hesitated, hating to drag the kids away. "Ben, Chris, as soon as that show's over I need you to come eat and help me feed the stock."

"We already did it," Ben told her, relieved that there would be no lecture on showing the proper respect for the furniture.

"You fed the stock already this morning?"

"And we had breakfast. Pancakes," Chris told her. "Dylan makes them real good."

"Oh." She stuck her hands in her pockets, feeling foolish and, worse, useless. "Then I'll heat up the coffee."

"Let me know how the planet makes out," Dylan said, then rose and followed Abby into the kitchen. "Problem?" he asked her.

"No." Just dozens of them, she thought as she turned the flame on under the pot. How was she supposed to keep promises to herself when she saw him playing with her children? How was she supposed to keep her mind busy when all the chores were done before she could even begin? No tenderness in him, no kindness—she needed to go on believing that if she wanted to stay whole.

She stiffened when he took her by the shoulders, but he ignored it and turned her to face him. With his eyes on hers, he put a hand to her forehead. "You still have a fever."

"I feel much better."

"You feel like hell," he said. Taking her by the arm, he led her to a stool. "Sit."

"Dylan, I'm used to running my own life."

"Fine. You should be able to get back to it by Monday."

"And what am I supposed to do until then?" The words came out in a heated rush as she gave in to her weakness and dropped down onto the stool. "I'm tired of lying in bed and eating soup. I'm tired of having a thermometer stuck in my mouth and aspirin poured down my throat."

"One of the first signs of getting well is crankiness." He set a glass of juice in front of her. "Drink."

"You're good at giving orders."

"You're lousy at taking them."

She scowled at him, then picked up the juice and drained it. "There. Satisfied?"

Not certain whether he should be amused or annoyed, Dylan skirted the counter. "What's eating you?"

"I've just told you. I . . ." Her voice trailed off as he took her face in his hand.

"You haven't told me half of it. But you will." Unable to resist, he stroked his thumb along her cheekbone.

"Don't." She lifted a hand to his wrist but couldn't make herself push him aside.

"People are my speciality," he murmured. "So far, I'm having a hard time getting through to what makes you tick. Do you like challenges, Abby?"

"No." She said it almost desperately. "No, I don't."

"I do." He combed his other hand through her hair, which was still damp from the shower. "I find them intriguing, and in some cases very arousing." He'd thought about her during the night. Thought about her and what he wanted. The more he thought, the more he believed the two might be the same thing. He touched his mouth to hers, just enough to awaken her. "You arouse me, Abby. What the hell are we going to do about that?"

"Stop." She fought to keep a tight hold on her emotions but her grip kept slipping. "The children."

"If they haven't seen their mother kissing a man before, they should have." The hand in her hair grew firmer. This time his mouth didn't merely touch hers, it absorbed it.

His lips were softer than they should have been, warmer, more...patient. None of it was expected. Was this how a man kissed a woman he desired, a woman he cared for? Was this what she'd been missing in her life, what she'd been craving without understanding? If it was, she wouldn't be able to fight it for long. Gentleness shattered her defenses in a way demands never could. Slowly, reluctantly, she opened to him. If her head was spinning it was the fever. She needed the excuse.

He couldn't explain the sense of innocence he felt from her, but it excited him. He couldn't explain his own sudden need, but it churned through him. He wanted her, alone. He wanted to see that look of panic and passion in her eyes when he touched her. He wanted to feel that slow, gradual melting of her body against his—half reluctant, half eager. He wanted to hear that quickening of breath that meant she'd forgotten everything but him. Whatever game she was playing, whatever lies she told, didn't matter when her mouth yielded to his.

He'd have his answers. He'd have hers. At the moment, he didn't care which came first.

"I want to take you to bed." He murmured it against her mouth, then against her skin as his lips skimmed over her face. "Soon, Abby, very soon."

"Dylan, I—"

"Are you taking Mom's temperature?"

Abby jerked back and stared, speechless, at Chris. He looked at her and at Dylan with the open, friendly curiosity that was an innate part of him.

"Mom kisses my forehead sometimes when I have a fever. Can I have a drink?"

"Yes." Abby fumbled for words while Chris found a glass. "Dylan was just—"

"Telling your mother she should get back in bed," Dylan finished for her. "And you and Ben need your coats. We have to run into town."

"Into town?" When she looked at him, she saw only cool amusement. She knew she should have expected that.

"We're out of a few things," he said easily enough. And he needed to get out, away from her, until he had himself back in order.

"Can I have some gum? Sugarless," Chris added, remembering his mother.

"Probably."

Leaving half a glass of juice on the counter, Chris went running for his brother.

"You don't have to take them," Abby began.

"I like the company."

Amusement helped fade the tension. "Oh, you'll have plenty of that. Have you ever taken two boys to the store?"

"I told you." He wasn't smiling now. "I like challenges."

"Yes, you did." Struggling to be calm, Abby rose. "They'll try to talk you into buying twice as much as you need."

"I'm a rock."

"Don't say I didn't warn you."

Then Ben and Chris came barreling in again, ready for the next adventure.

Abby compromised with herself. She did indeed have work to do and barely enough energy to stand. In order to accomplish some of the first and give in to the second, she took her paperwork to bed with her. The least she could do was pay the bills and bring her account and checkbooks up-to-date.

Because the house was quiet, she turned on the radio beside the bed before she began. Though she'd long ago accepted it as an unending cycle, it continued to give Abby a sense of satisfaction to pay bills and diminish the amount of her debts.

The house came first, and always would. It was security for her family and, undeniably, for herself. Fourteen years and two months to go, she mused as she sealed the envelope.

Fourteen years, she thought again. Her boys would be men. She wanted the home where they'd grown up to matter, to be full of good memories, love, laughter and a balancing sense of responsibility. That wasn't something she could give them merely by writing a check. That was something else she wanted them to grow to understand. What you had wasn't nearly as important as what you were. There were those, she knew, who never found the serenity to understand that.

She wrote her monthly check to Grover Stanholz with a mixture of gratitude and resentment—gratitude to the man for the loan, resentment that the loan itself had been necessary. Resentment didn't help, she reminded herself. Fulfilling the obligation would. Her answer there was the foals. If their price was right, she'd have come a long way toward being free of at least one of her obligations. Settling back, Abby wrote the note she always attached to the check.

Dear Grover,

   I hope this finds you well and happy. The children are great and looking forward, as I am, to the end of winter. The weather's finally beginning to clear up, though there are a few patches of snow and ice here and there. I want to thank you again for the invitation to join you in Florida. I know the boys would have enjoyed a few days, but it just wasn't possible to leave the farm or take them out of school.

Two of our mares are nearly ready to foal. Spring promises to be exciting. If you consider a trip north, please come. I'd like you to see what you helped me accomplish.

As always,
Abby

It never seemed enough. Abby folded the letter and sighed. There was so little she could say. She could have mentioned Dylan. They had discussed their joint contribution to the book and she knew that Dylan had already interviewed him. Somehow, she thought, it would help both of them to avoid the subject until it was all finished. Stanholz had loved Chuck like a father and had grieved like one. It seemed she could do no more than send him pictures of the children a couple times a year and a tidy note attached to a check once a month.

Shaking off the mood, she continued to sort through bills. Some she could pay, some she knew she had to put off just a little while longer. When she was finished, she had a grand total of $27.40 in her checking account.

So she'd dip into the emergency fund, she told herself. That was what emergency funds were for. The boys were going to need new shoes within the month, and twenty-seven dollars wasn't going to do it. It only proved she'd made the right decision in agreeing to the book. With that money to fall back on, she could keep everything afloat. When the foals were born . . .

She had to stop. Abby closed the books firmly and tidied the papers. She wasn't going to fall into the trap of thinking about money every waking moment. There would be enough. That was all she needed to know.

Laying back, she frowned at the ceiling. Want to or not, she didn't think she had the strength to tackle the kitchen floor or any of the other heavy household chores on her list for the day. But she wasn't going to vegetate, either. When was the last time she'd had a Saturday free? Thinking of it made her laugh at herself. And how many times had she wished for one so she could do nothing at all? Well, she'd gotten her wish, and she hated it.

Turning her head, she spotted the thermometer. She refused to touch it. But beside it was the phone. Abby hesitated, then reached for it. She'd just paid most of the bills, hadn't she? What better time for a little extravagance?

Abby dialed the phone, then waited impatiently until the third ring.

"Hi."

Just hearing the syllable made her smile. "Maddy."

"Abby!" The rest of the words tumbled out quickly, as though Maddy wanted to hurry them aside so she could say something else. "Terrific. I was just thinking about you. Must be another triplet flash. What's going on?"

"I've got the flu and I'm feeling sorry for myself."

"Now you don't have to. I'll feel sorry for you. Are you getting plenty of rest and liquids? I bet you've never taken one of those megavitamins I sent."

"Yes, I did." She'd taken a total of five before they'd ended up in the back of a cupboard. "Anyway, I'm feeling a bit better today."

Maddy stepped over a boot and sat on a pile of magazines. "How are the monsters?"

"Wonderful. They hate school, very often hate each other, never pick up anything and make me laugh at least six times a day."

"You're lucky."

"I know. Tell me about New York, Maddy. I want to get away for a while."

"We had some snow last week. It was beautiful." Maddy rarely noticed how quickly it turned to gray sludge. "On my day off I walked through Central Park. It was just like fairyland. Even the muggers were charmed."

There was no use telling Maddy it might not be wise to walk through fairyland alone. "How's the play going?"

"Looks like it could run forever. Did you know Mom and Pop made a swing through here last month? They had a couple of gigs in the Catskills and I talked them into a detour through Manhattan. Pop had this terrific argument with the choreographer."

"I bet he did. How are they?"

"The older we get, the younger they get. I don't know how it works." The pause was so slight that no one but her sister would have detected it. "Abby, did you go ahead with the book?"

"Yes." She concentrated on keeping her tone easy. "As a matter of fact, the writer's already here."

"Everything okay?"

"Everything's fine."

"I wished you'd waited until one of us could have been there with you."

"That's silly. But I do miss you—you and Chantel and Mom and Pop. And Trace."

"I got a telegram."

"From Trace? Where is he?"

"Morocco. He wanted me to know he'd shown my picture to some sheikh and got an offer of twelve camels for me. Pretty exciting."

"Did he take it?"

"I wouldn't be surprised. Abby, I'm thinking about leaving the show."

"Leaving? But you just said it could run forever."

"Yeah, that's why. It's getting too easy. I've been with it for a year now." Poking at the table beside her, Maddy found an earring she'd been certain had been lost forever. Without giving it a thought, she clipped it on. "I think it might be time to move on to something else. If I do, would you mind company for a few days?"

"Oh, Maddy, I'd love it."

"Well, keep the light burning, kid. I've got to go. Saturday matinee. Give my love to the boys."

"I will. Bye."

Abby sat back and pictured her sister grabbing her bag, searching for her keys, then dashing out of her apartment, already ten minutes late for makeup. That was Maddy's style. She had a critically acclaimed Broadway musical under her belt and was thinking of leaving it to see what was around the corner. That, too, was Maddy's style.

And hers was to do the laundry. With a little sigh, Abby got out of bed.

An hour later, she was satisfied she had some portion of her life under control. Dressed in baggy sweats, she carried the first load of clean, folded laundry toward the stairs. The front door burst open and two boys and a dog bounded in.

"Sigmund!" She made a quick evasive maneuver before the dog could knock her and the fresh linen to the floor.

"Mom, Mom! I got a new truck." Thrilled with himself, Chris brandished a shiny new pickup as he shouted over a mouthful of gum.

"Hey, very fancy." She set her basket down to examine it from hood to taillights as she knew was expected of her.

"I got a plane." Ben was bouncing up and down to get her attention. "A jet."

"Let's see." Abby took it and duly gave it the once-over. "Looks pretty fast. Where's—"

Dylan walked through the door, a bag of groceries under each arm. "More bags in the car, fellas."

"Okay!" They tore out again, the dog at their heels.

"A rock, huh?" Abby smiled at him as he walked past her.

"Aren't you supposed to be in bed?"

"I was. Now I'm not." She followed him into the kitchen. "Dylan, it was very nice of you to buy things for the boys, but you shouldn't let them pressure you."

"Easy for you to say," he muttered. He wasn't quite ready to admit the pleasure it had given him to buy a couple of plastic toys. "I did pretty well, all in all. I think Ben wanted an atomic bomb."

"It was on his Christmas list." She poked in the first bag and pulled out a box of little vanilla cakes with cream filling. "Twinkies?"

"I happen to like Twinkies."

"Mmm. And chocolate ice-cream bars."

"And chocolate ice-cream bars," he agreed, snatching them out of her hand.

"Got any teeth left?"

"Keep it up and I'll show you."

"And guess what else?" Chris staggered into the room under the weight of a grocery bag. Abby saved the bag, set it on the counter, then scooped him up.

"What else?"

"We have a surprise." He hooked his feet behind her waist and laughed.

"You're not supposed to tell." Ben walked in, trying not to show the strain as he carried the last bag.

"I see. Well, it seems to me that anyone who worked so hard must be ready for lunch."

"We ate already." Ben set his bag down and eyed the box of Twinkies. "Hamburgers."

"And French fries," Chris added.

"Sounds like quite a day."

"It was neat. I want to put the stickers on my plane now. Come on, Chris."

At the imperial order, Chris was scrambling down and racing after his brother.

"Don't walk much, do they?" Dylan commented as he stashed the groceries away.

"I guess you found that out in the store." She started to empty bags but she was more interested in Dylan. "I'm a little surprised," she began. "You don't look ready for a bottle of aspirin and a nap."

"Should I be?"

"I don't know. Actually, you look as if you enjoyed yourself."

"I did." He closed a cupboard door and turned. "Surprised?"

"Yes." Chuck had never enjoyed them. He'd been frustrated, baffled and annoyed by them and he'd never enjoyed them. "Most men—bachelors—don't consider an afternoon shopping with kids a barrel of laughs."

"You generalize."

She moved her shoulders dismissively. "I suppose I've never asked if you have children of your own."

"No. My ex-wife was a model. She wasn't ready to take time out for children."

"I'm sorry."

He turned, giving her a mild, half-amused look. "For what?"

The question left her stumbling. "Divorce—it's usually a difficult experience."

"In this case, marriage was the difficult experience. It only lasted a year and a half."

Such a short time, she thought. Yet he did seem like a man who would admit a mistake quickly and deal with it. "But still, divorce is never pleasant."

"And marriage rarely is."

She opened her mouth to disagree but discovered she had very little ammunition. "But divorce is like admitting you're a failure, isn't it?"

She wasn't talking about him. He took a gallon of milk and put it in the refrigerator, wondering if she knew how transparent she was. "The marriage was a failure. I wasn't."

She shrugged off the feeling. In the way he'd seen his own mother do, she neatly folded the empty bags. "I suppose it's easier when children aren't involved."

"I wouldn't know about that. I'd say when a marriage is bad, it's bad. It doesn't do anyone any good to pretend otherwise."

She glanced up to see him staring at her. Too close to the bone, Abby thought, keeping her hands busy. "Well, we seem to have things under control here."

"Not yet. But nearly." He crossed over and put his hand to her brow. "Fever's down."

"I told you I was feeling better."

"Good. Because I want you to have all your strength back before we start again. I like to play fair whenever possible."

"And when it's not?"

"Then it's not. Do you believe in rules, Abby?"

"Of course."

"There's no 'of course.' People make rules, then they use them or they ignore them. Smart people don't box themselves in with them. I've got to get something else out of the car."

Dissatisfied with him and with the situation, Abby went back and picked up the laundry. She heard the boys shuffling around in Ben's room and went into her own.

How much did Dylan suspect about her marriage? She hadn't intended to make it sound as though it had been made in heaven. Or had she? She'd wanted to give the illusion of normalcy, of contentment. The agreement with herself had been made. There would be no mention of the tears and broken promises, of the lies and disillusionment. She would never have been able to hide the infidelities already gleefully recorded in the scandal sheets, but she'd thought she could play them down. And never, never had it occurred to her that he might discover that divorce papers had been filed weeks before Chuck's last race.

He probably didn't know, she told herself as she walked to the window and looked out over her land. He would have no reason to question her lawyer. And if he did, wasn't that privileged information? Four years earlier she'd agonized over how to tell her children she was divorcing their father. Instead, she'd had to tell them their father was dead.

Chris hadn't understood. He'd barely known who his father was and hadn't comprehended death at all. But Ben had. They'd wept together, and that first night they'd lain together in the bed where she'd spent so many other nights alone.

Now she was trying to give them what she felt they needed to understand their father and themselves. And she had to protect them. The problem was, she was no longer so sure she could do both.

"Mom." Ben pushed open her door without knocking. "You've got to come down. The surprise is ready."

She looked at him as he stood in the doorway, eager, flushed with excitement and miserably untidy. "Ben." She walked over and caught him up in a fierce hug. "I love you."

Pleased, embarrassed, he laughed a little. And since there was no one to see, he hugged her back as hard as he could. "I love you, Mom."

Then, because she knew him, she nuzzled into his neck until he squealed. "What's the surprise?" she demanded.

"I'm not telling."

"I can make you talk. I can make you beg to tell me everything you know."

"Mom!" Chris yelled impatiently from the bottom of the stairs. "Come down, we can't start till you're here, Dylan says."

Dylan says, she thought with a sigh. Taking advantage of her momentary distraction, Ben squirmed away and danced to the stairs. "Hurry," he ordered, then bolted downstairs.

Amused, Abby started after him. "Okay, where is everybody?" She found them in the living room, huddled over a VCR. "What's this?"

"Dylan rented it." Chris, nearly delirious with pleasure, climbed onto the couch and bounced. "You play tapes of movies on it."

"I know." She glanced at Dylan as he handily attached the necessary plugs.

"He said since we couldn't go to the movies we could have them at home. We got *Warriors in Space*."

She caught Chris on an upswing. *"Warriors in Space?"*

"I was outvoted," Dylan told her. "They had some very interesting movies in the back room."

"I bet they did."

"I did pick up this as well." He tossed her a second tape.

"Lawless," she murmured. "Chantel's big break. She was really wonderful in this movie."

"I've always been partial to it."

"I still remember sitting in the theater and watching her come on the screen. It was an incredible feeling." Just holding the tape brought her sister closer and reminded her that she was never really alone. "It's funny, I just talked to Maddy a couple of hours ago, and now—"

"Can we watch Chantel, too?" Ben was nearly beside himself with the idea of such extravagance. "I like to see when she shoots the guy in the hat."

She hesitated, struggling with a feeling of obligation she didn't know what to do with. Both boys looked at her with eager impatience. Dylan simply lifted a brow and waited. She gave in, as much for herself, she realized, as for anyone else.

"Seems to me we should have popcorn."

He grinned, understanding very well the process that had gone on inside her head. "You up to making it?"

"Oh, I think I can manage."

Twenty minutes later they were spread out on the sofa, watching the first in a series of flashy laser battles. Ben, as usual, was rooting ferociously for the bad guys. Chris's little fingers tensed on Abby's arm, and she leaned down and whispered something that made him laugh.

It was so normal. That was what kept running through her head as the movie rolled noisily on. Watching movies and eating homemade popcorn on a chilly Saturday afternoon—it seemed so easy, almost nonsensically easy, but she'd really never wanted much else. Relaxed, Abby draped her arm on the back of the sofa. Her hand brushed Dylan's. She started to draw away, then glanced over at him.

He watched her over the heads of her sons. The questions that always seemed to be in his eyes were still there, but she was growing accustomed to them. And to him. He had done this for her, for her children. Maybe, just maybe, he'd done it for himself, as well. Maybe that was all that really mattered. With a smile, she linked her fingers with his.

He wasn't used to such simplicity from a woman. She'd just smiled and taken his hand. There had been no flirtation in the gesture, no subtle promises. If he'd been willing to take the gesture at face value, he'd have said it was a simple thank-you.

He thought this must be what it was like to have a family. Not-so-quiet weekends with sticky faces and mundane chores and a living room littered with toys. Warm smiles from a woman who seemed happy to have you there. Dozens of questions that leaped out of young minds and demanded answers. And contentment, the kind that didn't require hot lights and fast music.

He'd always wanted a family. Once he'd told himself he wanted Shannon more—Shannon with the slim, amazing body and the dark, sultry looks. She'd touched off things inside him—exploded was more accurate, Dylan admitted. He found it much easier to remember now than it once had been. They'd met, made love and married, all in a whirling sexual haze. It had seemed right. They'd both lived on the edge and enjoyed it. Somehow it had been incredibly wrong. She'd wanted more, more money, more excitement, more glamour. He'd wanted... He was damned if he knew what he'd wanted.

But if he could believe the woman sitting two children away from him was real, it might be her.

Chapter Seven

A backlog of work had helped Abby avoid Dylan throughout the morning. His typewriter had been clicking when she'd woken the boys for school. It had clattered steadily, almost routinely, rather than in the quick on-again, off-again spurts of creation she'd expected. Perhaps it was routine for him, digging into and recording the lives of other people.

The sound had reminded her forcibly that the weekend had only been a reprieve. It was Monday, she was recovered, and the questions were about to begin again. She wished she could recapture the confidence of a week ago and believe she could answer only the ones she chose to, and answer them in her own way.

Still, her own routine soothed her—the breakfast clatter, the scent of coffee, the typically frantic search for a lost glove before she sent her sons racing off to catch the bus. She watched them go down the lane as she did every morning. It struck her, unexpectedly and sharply, as it did now and then, that they were hers. *Hers.* Those two apprentice men in wool caps heading off to face the day at a fast trot had come from her. It was fascinating, wonderful and just a little frightening.

When they disappeared, she continued to watch a little longer. Whatever happened, whatever strange twist life tossed at her, no one could take away the wonder of her children. The day no longer seemed so hard to face.

As she headed toward the barn a few minutes later, she heard the sound of a car. Changing direction, she walked around the side and saw Mr. Petrie hopping out of the cab of his truck. She could have kissed his grizzled face.

"Ma'am." He grinned at her, then spit out a plug of tobacco.

"Mr. Petrie, I'm so glad to see you." She shifted the bucket of eggs as she studied him. "Are you sure you're well enough to work?"

"Right as rain."

He did look fit. His small, stubby body appeared well fed. Beneath several days' growth of beard, his color was good, ruddy, windburned and reliable. He was hardly taller than she and built somewhat like a thumb—sturdy and unexpectedly agile. The boots he wore were black and worn and tied up over his ankles. "If your wife let you out of the house, I guess you're ready to pitch some hay."

"Old nag," he said affectionately. "She kept a mustard plaster on me for a week." His small, slightly myopic eyes narrowed. "You look a might peaked."

"No, I'm fine. I was just about to get started in the barn."

"How are the ladies?"

"Wonderful." They began to walk together over the slowly drying ground. "The vet was here on Friday and gave them both a checkup. It looks like Eve and Gladys are going to be mothers before the week's out."

Petrie spit again as they crossed to the barn. "Jorgensen came by?"

"Yes, he's very interested."

"Don't let that old horse thief buffalo you. Top dollar." Petrie swung the door open with a hand that was missing the first knuckle of the ring finger.

"No one's going to buffalo me," she assured him.

He'd known her five years and worked for her for nearly two, and he believed her. She might look like something out of one of the magazines his wife kept on the coffee table, but she was tough. A woman alone had to be. "Tell you what now, you take the horses out and groom them. I'll clean out the stalls."

"But—"

"No, now you've been swinging a pitchfork on your own all last week. Looks like you need some sun to me. 'Sides, I gotta work off some of this food my wife pushed on me when I was too weak to stop her. There now, sweetheart." He stroked Eve's head when she leaned it over the stall. His ugly, callused hands were as gentle as a lute player's. "Old Petrie's back." He pulled out a carrot and let her take it from his hand.

Abby appreciated his easy touch with the horses, just as she had always relied on his judgment. "She's missed you."

"Sure she has." He moved down to the next stall and gave the second mare equal attention. "I tell you something, Miz Rockwell, if I had the means I'd have myself a mare like this."

She knew the position he was in, knew the limitations of living off social security and little else. The regret that she couldn't pay him more came quickly, as it always did. "I wouldn't have either of them if you hadn't helped me."

"Oh, you'd've got by all right—but maybe you'd've paid too much." With a cackle, he went down to the next horse. "You were a novice back then, Miz Rockwell, but I think you've lost your green."

From him, it was an incredible compliment. With more pleasure than she'd been able to drum up in days, Abby began to lead the horses out. She groomed them in the sunshine.

Dylan watched her from his window. She was singing. He couldn't hear her, but he could tell by the way she moved. He watched as she meticulously cleaned out hooves, brushed manes and curried. There was a lightness about her that he hadn't seen before. But then, she thought she was alone.

Her gloves were on a post, and she ran her bare hands over the flank of one of the geldings. Tea-serving hands, he thought. Yet somehow they looked just as right brushing hard over the gelding's coat. How would they look brushing over his skin? How would it feel to have those hands running with abandon over his body, arousing, exciting, exploring? Would she have that dreamy look in her eyes? He thought she had it now, but he was too far away to be certain.

And if he was smart, he'd stay away.

Her face wouldn't be pale now. The early-morning air would bring the color up as the strong sunlight and exercise warmed her muscles. Her face wouldn't be pale when he made love with her. Excitement would flush it. Passion would make her agile. He could imagine what it would be like to have her skin slide over his. He could almost taste the flavor of her flesh in those dark, secret places made only more mysterious by the layers of thick winter clothing. He wanted to peel them off her while she stood watching him, wanting him, waiting for him. Just thinking of it made his pulse thud.

He'd wanted other women. Sometimes his wants had been eased, sometimes they hadn't. Passion came and passion went. It erupted and it vanished. He understood that well. Just because he churned for her now, just because he stood at the window and watched her with needs bouncing crazily inside him that didn't mean he'd want her tomorrow. Desire couldn't rule your life—not desire for money, not for power and certainly not for a woman.

But he continued to watch her while his typewriter hummed impatiently behind him.

He watched as she led the horses, two and three at a time, into the barn. He waited until she came out again not even calculating the time that passed. Then, abruptly and obviously on impulse, she swung herself onto the big gelding she'd called Judd. With a halter and nothing else, she sent the horse racing out of the paddock and up the rough, narrow track that led in to the hills.

He wanted to throw the window open and yell at her not to be an idiot. He wanted to watch her ride. He could see her knees pressed tight to the gelding's side and her hand holding the halter rope. But more, as the sun fell like glory over her face, he saw the look of absolute delight.

She let the gelding run up and down the track—ten minutes, fifteen, Dylan was too mesmerized to notice. Her hair rose and fell in the wind they created, but she never bothered to push it from her face. And when she swung to the ground he knew she was laughing. She nuzzled the horse, stroking again. Stroking, soothing, murmuring. Dylan wondered what soft, pretty words she spoke.

A man was losing his grip when he became jealous of a horse. He knew it but continued to stand by the window, straining for control, or perhaps for the inevitable. She disappeared inside the barn again, and he told himself to turn away, to get back to his work, but he waited.

She returned with the stallion, holding the rope close under his chin as he danced impatiently, bad-temperedly. Abby tied him securely to the rail and began to groom him.

The animal was beautiful, his head thrown high and an arrogant look in his eyes that Dylan could see even from the window. And he was skittish. When Abby took his hind leg to clean his hoof, he jerked it twice, nearly pulling out of her grip before he settled down and let her do her business. When she set it down again, Dylan caught his breath as the horse took a hard, nasty kick at her. Abby avoided it and calmly picked up the next leg. He could almost hear her gently scolding as she might have if one of the boys had had a fit of temper.

Damn it, who are you? He pressed a hand to the glass as if demanding she look up, hear him and answer. Who the hell are you? If she was genuine, why the lies? If she had the kind of morals, the kind of values she seemed to have, how could she lie?

Yet she was lying, Dylan reminded himself. And she would continue to lie until he tripped her up. Today, he promised himself as he watched her brush out the smooth, dark skin of the stallion. Today, Abby.

Turning, he went back to his typewriter and told himself to forget her.

It was after eleven when he heard her come back into the house. He had Rockwell's early professional years, his earlier family background, drafted out. He'd written of Rockwell's meeting with Abby from her perspective, using quotes from her and bits of her family history. People would be interested in the sister of one of Hollywood's rising stars, and in the sister of a successful Broadway actress. He hadn't overlooked the triplet angle or the theater background. Three sisters, three actresses. But he was about to rewrite Abby's script.

She heard him come down but continued to wash the eggs. "Good morning." She didn't look back at him, and continued to keep her hands busy. "Coffee's on."

"Thanks."

When he walked to the stove, she glanced over. He hadn't shaved. It always made her stomach quiver—perhaps at the thought of having that rough, slightly uncivilized face scrape against hers.

"Mr. Petrie's back. I think he could have used another day or two, but he missed the horses."

"You finished out there?"

"For now. I'm going to be checking on the mares off and on."

"Fine." He took his coffee to the bar, lit a cigarette, then turned on his tape recorder. "When did you and Rockwell decide to divorce?"

An egg hit the floor with a splat. Abby stared down at it in dull surprise. Without a word, she began to clean it up.

"Do you want me to repeat the question?"

"No." Her voice was muffled, then came stronger. "No, but I would be interested to know where you got the idea."

"Lori Brewer."

"I see." Abby cleaned up the last of the mess, then turned to wash her hands.

"She was sleeping with your husband."

"I'm aware of that." Abby dried her hands meticulously. They were steady. She hung on to that.

"She wasn't the first."

"I'm also aware of that." She went to the stove and poured coffee.

"You got ice for blood, lady?" When she turned to look at him calmly, it goaded him all the more. "Your husband slept with any woman who could crawl between the sheets. He made a career out of cheating on you. Lori Brewer was only the last in a long line."

Did he think she was hurting her? she wondered. Did he think she should feel a stab of pain, a wave of betrayal? She'd felt it all before, but that was long since over. She felt nothing now but a sort of vague curiosity about the anger she saw in Dylan's eyes.

"If we both know that, why talk about it?"

"Was he going to dump you for her?"

She took a sip of coffee. It steadied the nerves. She would give him the truth as long as it was possible to give him the truth. "Chuck never asked me for a divorce." She drank again, and the liquid slipped, hot and potent, into her system. "Though he may very well have told Lori Brewer that he did."

That was the truth. His gut told him that this time she spoke with pure honesty. It only made it more of a morass. "She's not a stupid woman. She had it in her head that she and Rockwell would be married before the year was out."

"I can't really comment on what she thought."

"What can you comment on?" His anger surged, and because he trusted it, he moved with it. Perhaps with anger he could finally break through her shield. "Tell me this—how did it feel knowing your husband wasn't faithful to you?"

She'd known the question would come up. She'd prepared herself for it. But now, somehow, the answer didn't come as easily. "Chuck and I...understood each other." How flat that sounded, how foolishly sophisticated. "I...well I knew he was under a great deal of pressure, and being on the road like that month after month..."

"...is a license to relieve the pressure anyway you chose?"

She wasn't as calm as she wanted to be, but she was still in control. "I'm not talking about a license, or even an excuse, Dylan. But it is a reason."

"You consider being separated from you, being on the road and pressured by a need to win, is a reason for the women, the booze, the drugs?"

"Drugs?" Her face went a dead white. If the shock in her eyes wasn't real, Dylan decided, she should be the sister in Hollywood. "I don't know what you're talking about."

"I'm talking about cocaine. Freebasing." His voice was clipped and hard, a reporter's voice. He tried not to hate himself for it.

"No." There was a sudden sheen of desperation in her voice. He watched her knuckles blanch as she gripped the counter. "No, I don't believe that."

"Abby, I have it from four different sources." His tone had softened. She was hurting inside. She might have lied to him before, but the pain was real. "You didn't know."

"You can't write that. You can't. The children." She put her hands over her eyes. "Oh, God, what I have done?"

He had her arm. She hadn't heard him get up. "Sit down." When she started to shake her head, he pulled her over to a stool. "Sit down, Abby."

"You can't write that," she repeated, and her voice was a roller coaster of ups and downs. "You can't be sure it's true. If you try to put that in the book, I'll withdraw my authorization. I'll sue."

"What you'd better do right now is calm down."

"Calm down?" She clutched her hands together until her fingers ached. Only determination kept her facing him, and her eyes were drenched with despair. "You've just told me that Chuck was—" She swallowed and got a grip on herself. "Turn that off," she said quietly, then waited until the recorder stopped. "We're off the record now, do you understand me?"

Her eyes were dry again and her voice steady. He had a sudden flash of her carrying his suitcase up the stairs. Stronger than she looked. "All right, Abby. Off the record."

"If Chuck—if he used drugs, I never knew."

"Do you think you would have?"

She closed her eyes. A sense of failure reached up and grabbed her by the throat. "No."

"I'm sorry." He touched her hand, swearing at himself when she drew back. "I am sorry. His mother knew. I have it that she tried to get him into rehab."

A sudden hysterical thought drummed through her. "The last race. The crash."

"He was clean." He thought he heard the relief sweep through her, though she didn't make a sound. "He just took the turn too fast."

She nodded and straightened her shoulders. If Abby had learned anything over the past eight years, it was to take one step at a time, deal with it, then go on. "Dylan I'm not asking for favors, but I'd like you to remember there are two innocent people involved. The children deserve some legacy from their father. If you try to print anything about this I'll find a way to stop you, even if I have to go to Janice."

"How much will you try to cover up, Abby?"

She gave him a clear, direct look. "You'd do better to ask me how much I'd do to protect my children."

He felt a twinge and fought to grind it down. "Once a ball's rolling, it rolls. You'd have been smarter to stop the book in the beginning."

"Isn't the sex enough for you?" she lashed out, desperate to find solid ground again. How could she take the first step when each time she did she was knee-deep in quicksand? "Do you have to put this ugly business in, too? Can't you leave the boys something?"

"Do you want me to write a fairy tale?" He grabbed her wrists before she could push away from the counter. He should have resented her for making him feel responsible, yet he couldn't. She looked lost and helpless. "Abby, it's too late to stop the book now. The publishers would sue you, not the other way around. Talk to me, tell me the truth. Trust me to tell it."

"Trust you?" She stared at him, wishing she could see inside him, find some soft, giving spot. "I trusted myself and I've made a mess of it." Faced with the inevitable, she stopped resisting his hold on her hands. "I've got no choice, do I?"

"No."

She waited a moment until she was certain she was strong enough. "Turn your recorder back on." She withdrew from him, not by inches but by miles. As soon as the machine was running, Abby began speaking again. But she never looked at him. "Chuck never used drugs in my presence. We were married for four years, and I never saw him with drugs of any kind. As far as I'm concerned, he never used them at all. Chuck was an athlete, and he was very disciplined about his body."

"For most of your marriage, you only lived together for short periods."

"That's true. We each had certain responsibilities that kept things that way."

"It would seem to me that you had certain responsibilities that should have kept you together."

She would ignore that. She wouldn't wallow in guilt or in self-pity ever again. If the time had come to compromise herself, so be it. She'd take the lesser demon. "To go back to your earlier question, Chuck was often lonely. He was attractive and women were a part of the circuit."

"You accepted that?"

"I accepted that Chuck was not capable of being faithful. I realized that a marriage is the responsibility of two people. In certain areas, I wasn't able to give him what he needed."

"What are you talking about?"

Pride was brushed aside. Abby had found it was rarely useful in any case. "I was only eighteen when we were married. Despite the fact that we were entertainers and on the road continually, I was very sheltered. I was a virgin when I married Chuck, and he often said I remained one. I failed him in bed and so he looked elsewhere. Maybe that was wrong, but it was also natural."

"Stop humiliating yourself this way."

She heard the barely restrained fury and turned to look at him. "You wanted answers, I'm giving them to you. Chuck slept with other women because his wife didn't satisfy him."

"The hell with this." He spun her on the stool until she faced him. "You're a fool if you believe that."

"Dylan, I know what went on in my own bedroom. You don't."

"I know what goes on inside you."

"You asked me if I had ice for blood. I'm answering you."

"No, you're not." He pulled her off the stool to stand beside him. "Now you will."

He had her close. His mouth came down on hers, hot, furious, before she could even think about protesting. Excitement bubbled up inside her to war with a strong desire for self-preservation. She tried to resist. There was something wild and frightening about the way he could take her over, make her hurt with need. The hands in her hair weren't gentle, but held her to him in a kind of angry possession. Slowly, inevitably, she let herself go.

He'd burned for her through the night, through the morning, but he hadn't expected it to be like this. There were waves of fire and smoke blinding him. Her body was tight as a bowstring against his, holding back against the passion he could feel building. Her fingers didn't push at his shoulders, but dug into them. He could almost hear her heart thudding in her throat—

fear, excitement, desire, he didn't care. As long as it was for him.

Then, with incredible ease, she relaxed. Her lips softened, her body yielded, and she was his.

Her heartbeat didn't slow. Somehow it increased even as her arms wound slowly around him. She sighed. He felt the soft trickle of air whisper against his mouth. He combed his hands through her hair, gently, soothingly, because she seemed to need it. The flame had gone out of him, but the heat was still there, simmering, sizzling. He could have burned alive with tenderness.

"Come upstairs, Abby." He murmured it against her ear, then against her mouth. "Come upstairs with me."

She wanted to. The fact that she did jolted her. She'd already accepted that she was attracted to him, but it was a different matter to slip into bed with a man. "Dylan, I—"

"I want you." His mouth loitered along her chin, where he bit gently. "You know that."

"I think I do. Please..." Her voice was trembling. Her muscles felt like putty. She couldn't allow herself to tumble over the edge a second time without keeping her eyes open. "Please, Dylan, I just can't. I'm not ready."

"You want me." He skimmed his hands up, molding her hips, tracing her ribs, teasing her breasts. "I can feel it every time you take a breath."

"Yes." She was through denying. "But I need more than that." She took his hand and brought it to her cheek. "I need some time."

Dylan brought his hand up under her chin and held it there. Her cheeks were flushed, as he'd once imagined they would be. Her eyes were dark and unsure. If it hadn't been for them, watching him, almost trusting him, he'd have ignored her protests and taken her.

"How badly did he mess up your head, I wonder."

"No." She shook her head. "This has nothing to do with what happened between Chuck and me."

"You don't believe that and neither do I. He's your yardstick. Sooner or later you're going to find out you can't measure me by it."

"I don't think of Chuck when I'm kissing you. I don't think at all."

His fingers tightened on her skin. "Abby, if you want time, you'd better watch yourself."

She felt the energy that had poured into her so quickly drain out again. "I don't know how to play the games, Dylan. That's the reason I messed up so badly once before."

"I'm not interested in games. And I'm not interested in hearing you shoulder blame. Let's make a deal."

She moistened her lips and wished she could be sure of herself again. "What sort?"

"You tell me the truth. The truth," he repeated, laying his hands on her shoulders. "I'll write it objectively. Then we'll let the blame fall wherever it belongs."

He made it sound so simple, but then he had nothing to lose. "I don't know if I can do that, Dylan. I have the children to think of. Sometimes the truth hurts."

"Sometimes it cleanses," he countered. "Abby, I'll find out everything I need to know one way or the other." It was a threat. He understood that, and he saw by the look that came and went in her eyes that she did, as well. "You should think about that. Don't you think it would be better if it came from you? I don't want to hurt those kids."

Trapped, she studied him, carefully, critically. "No, I don't think you do, but you and I might not agree on what's best for them."

He rubbed a hand over his face, then paced around the kitchen. It wasn't like him to make compromises. He didn't care for it. Yet he was compelled to find one. The book? He was beginning to think the book didn't mean much of anything. He wanted the truth from her, about her. And he wanted it for himself. He thought perhaps he wanted it for her.

"Okay, you give me the real story, the true story, without all the little evasions. I'll write it, and then before I submit anything for publication I'll give it to you to read. If there's a problem, we'll work it out. Both of us have to be satisfied with the manuscript before it flies."

She hesitated. "Do you mean that?"

He turned back. She wasn't ready to trust him. The woman had been lied to before, he thought, and lied to in a big way. "You've got it on record." He gestured to the recorder which was still running.

She took the step, though her legs were a little wobbly. "All right."

When he came forward and offered his hand, Abby held her breath and accepted it. Another bargain, she thought, hoping she could keep it better than the one she'd made with herself.

"He hurt you."

Dylan said it quietly, so quietly she answered without hesitation. "Yes."

It made him angry. No, it made him furious. He couldn't explain it, but he knew that fury wouldn't help him get to the truth. And for years, maybe too many years, that had been his driving ambition. "Why don't you sit down again?"

She nodded, then sat with her hands neatly folded and her face placid.

"Abby, you and Rockwell were having serious marital problems."

"That's right." It seemed so easy to say it now. Just as he'd said, cleansing.

"Was it the other women?"

"That was part of it. Chuck needed more than I could give him in so many areas. I guess I needed more than he could give me. He wasn't a bad man." The words were quick and earnest. "I want you to understand that. Maybe he wasn't a good husband, but he wasn't a bad man."

Dylan planned to use his own judgment there. "Why did you stop traveling with him?"

"I was pregnant with Ben." She let out a little breath. "I can't honestly say whether that was a convenient excuse or a legitimate reason, but I was pretty far along, and traveling had become difficult. We were living with his mother in Chicago. At first . . . at first he managed to fly back fairly often. I think he was happy, maybe a little awed at the idea of being a father. In any case, he was attentive when he was home, and he encouraged me to stay in Chicago and take care of myself. He tried, really tried to ease the uncomfortable relationship I had with his mother. There were long separations."

She looked back, remembering those weeks, months in the luxurious house in Chicago, long idle mornings, quiet afternoons. It seemed like a dream, one in soft focus but with surprisingly sharp edges.

"I was content and rather pleased with myself. I decorated the nursery and took up knitting . . . badly." She laughed at herself as she remembered her fumbling attempts. "I figured I had just about everything under control. Then one day I found one of those gossip papers on my bed. I've always wondered if Janice left it there." Abby shook that away, it hardly mattered. "There was a picture of Chuck and this really beautiful woman, and a short, nasty article."

She looked out the window and watched the trees bend a little. "I sat there, big and clumsy and nearly eight months pregnant. I was crushed and betrayed and absolutely certain the world was over. Chuck came home at the end of the week and I tossed the paper at him demanding an explanation."

"He gave you one."

"He was angry that I'd believe a story like that. He called it trash and threw it in the fire. He didn't defend himself, so I was abruptly in the position of apologizing. Do you understand?"

He thought he could picture her, fragile and alone. His anger only burned brighter. "Yeah, I understand."

"I was one month away from having a baby, and scared to death. I decided to believe him, but of course I knew, because I'd seen it in his face, that he was lying. I accepted the lie. Do you understand?" Why did she keep asking that? Why was it so important? She pressed her fingers against her eyes a moment and swore not to ask again. "I think by accepting it I only hurt him."

"You believe if you'd had a showdown then it would have stopped."

Her eyes were solemn. "I'll never be sure."

"And there were other women."

"There were others. Remember that Chuck and I weren't living together under normal circumstances and that our physical relationship had deteriorated. He was a man who needed victories, but as soon as he'd achieved them, he needed more. If you could try to understand that even as a child he was under tremendous pressure to succeed, to be the best—to be number one.''

Weary of it all, she let out a little sigh. "Because of that, he required constant reassurance that he was the greatest. After a while, I don't think I gave him that. In any case, I'd thought—hoped—that after Ben was born we'd settle down. But I knew, or should have known, when I married Chuck, that he was far from ready to settle. There was an ugly little scandal with one of the groupies. She wrote me letters, threatened to kill herself if Chuck didn't marry her. That's when we bought this place. Chuck was upset because things had gotten out of hand. It was an attempt to make it up to me, to Ben, maybe to himself. But then there was another race.''

"You didn't go with him.''

"No. For a while I concentrated on making a home. I felt he needed one. The fact was, I needed one.'' She watched the smoke from Dylan's cigarette curl slowly toward the ceiling. "During that time, after Ben was born and before I became pregnant with Chris, I began to realize that our marriage wasn't working, that Chuck and I were only pretending it had ever worked. He came home. He'd won in Italy. He wanted to sell the farm. We had a terrible fight about it. While we were fighting, Ben toddled in. Chuck just went wild. He yelled at Ben, who was crying.''

She dragged a hand through her hair as the misery of that memory came back to her. "Ben was barely a year old. I lost my temper and told Chuck to get out. He got in his car and went tearing up the road. I calmed Ben down and finally got him to sleep.

"It was late and I went to bed. I didn't expect Chuck to came back, I didn't care. But he came back." Her voice had dropped almost to a whisper. As he watched her, Dylan realized she wasn't talking to him any longer. She was exorcizing her own ghosts. "He'd been drinking. He never drank very much because he couldn't handle it well, but this time he'd been drinking heavily. He came upstairs and we argued again. I was trying to get him to go sleep in one of the guest rooms so he wouldn't disturb Ben. He was too furious and too drunk to listen to reason. He said I'd never been any kind of wife, and less of a lover. He said I only cared about Ben and the farm. God, it was true. It hadn't always been but he was right and I wouldn't admit it. He said it was about time I learned what it was a man wanted from his wife. What it was a man expected and was entitled to. So he shoved me back on the bed...and he raped me," she said flatly as Dylan stared at her. "Then he cried like a baby. He left before dawn. A few weeks later I found out I was pregnant."

Her hand trembled as she ran it through her hair. "That's honest, Dylan. That's the truth." She focused on him again. "Should I tell Chris that he was conceived the night his father forced himself on me? Is that the truth I owe my son?"

She didn't wait for him to answer, but stood slowly and walked out of the room.

Chapter Eight

He couldn't work. Dylan stared almost resentfully at his typewriter, but he couldn't bring himself to put words on paper. The words were there, jammed tight in his head. The emotion was there, still churning through him. He could remember, point by point, precisely what had happened throughout the afternoon and evening.

When Abby had walked out of the kitchen, he'd just sat there staring at the tape, which had continued to run. Shocked? How could he say he was shocked? He'd taken off his rose-colored glasses years before. He knew how ugly life could be, how violent, how petty. He'd chipped his way into lives before and found the sores, the scars and the secrets. They didn't shock him, and they had stopped affecting him a long time ago.

But he'd sat in the kitchen a long time, where the scent of coffee had still lingered. And he'd hurt. He'd hurt because he could remember how pale her face had been, how calm her voice had sounded when she'd told him. Then he'd left her alone, knowing privacy was what she'd wanted.

He'd driven into town. Distance, he'd told himself, would help. A journalist needed distance, just as he needed intimacy. It was the combination of the two that brought truth and power to a story. And wasn't it always the story that came first?

The air had warmed, though the wind was starting to kick up to welcome March. Snow was just a memory on the still-soggy ground. Spring was beginning to push its way through. And when spring faded the book should be finished. He no longer knew precisely how.

When he'd come back, the boys had been home from school. They'd been playing in the yard, racing with the dog and each other. Dylan had sat in the car for a few moments, watching them, until Chris had rushed over to invite him to play catch.

Even now, hours later, Dylan could remember just how bright Chris's face had been, how open and innocent his eyes had looked. The little hand had gripped his with absolute trust as he'd begun to ramble on about his day in school. Someone named Sean Parker had thrown up at recess. Big news. Ben had said something childishly obscene about Sean Parker's dilemma, and Chris had giggled until he'd been ready to burst.

They'd raced around the back and had barreled into the kitchen. Standing behind them, Dylan had seen Abby at the stove. When she'd turned, their eyes had held for one long moment. Then she'd fallen into the predinner routine with the easy efficiency he'd come to expect from her.

He'd waited for the tension, but it hadn't come, not then, not during dinner, not later when she'd played a board game with the children and he'd been drafted to join them. Normal was the order of the day, and if it was forced, even he couldn't tell. She'd seen the children off to bed, then had retreated to her room. She'd been there ever since.

In his own room, he found it impossible to get settled. What was he going to do? He had the makings of a tough, honest story in the palm of his hand. Romance, betrayal, sex, violence. And it wasn't fiction, it was real. It was his job to write it and to write it honestly, thoroughly.

He remembered how trustingly that small hand had fit into his.

Swearing, Dylan pushed away from his desk. He couldn't do it. It wasn't possible to put down in black and white what Abby had told him that afternoon. No matter how he wrote, no matter how carefully he phrased it, it would be ugly, hollow, unforgivable. And the child was so beautifully untouched and open.

It shouldn't matter. All the instincts that had driven him through his years of reporting, all the skill that had made his biographies hard-edged and genuine, pushed him to the truth. But he could remember the way a small boy had grinned and lifted his arms for a hug. He remembered Ben sitting alone and sulky on a bed surrounded by tiny men. And he remembered how Abby had linked her fingers with his and made him feel whole.

They'd gotten to him. Dylan dragged a hand through his hair. There was no use pretending otherwise. Inside him was a tug-of-war that they'd created and he was still fighting. He'd forgotten the cardinal rule, the one he'd learned in his first week as a pool reporter: don't get involved. Well, he was involved, and he had no idea how to draw back.

The hell with drawing back.

Without giving himself a chance to think it through, Dylan walked out of his room, crossed the hall and knocked on Abby's door.

"Yes, come in."

She was sitting at a small writing desk, finishing a letter. She glanced up, then set it aside as if she'd been expecting him.

"We need to talk."

"All right. Close the door."

He closed it, but he didn't speak at once. There was no barrier between them now, no recorder that made everything profession and ethical. What was said now would be between the two of them. Or more accurately, he realized, *for* the two of them. He wasn't certain how it had come down to this. Like a man walking down a dimly lit road, he walked over and sat on the bed.

The room was quiet, soft, feminine—as she was. If there had been violence here, it had long since been eradicated. She'd locked it away, he realized, because she wouldn't let her life or the lives of her children be destroyed by it. By putting the knowledge in his hands, she'd made him responsible. Something within her had reached in and discovered the compassion that made him accept the responsibility.

"Abby, you know I can't write what you told me this afternoon."

A wave of relief rolled over her. She'd hoped, she'd dared to trust, but she hadn't been sure. "Thank you."

"Don't be grateful." In some ways he felt he could deal with her resentment more successfully. "I'm going to write plenty that you won't like."

"I'm beginning to think it doesn't matter as much as I once believed it did." She looked beyond him to the tiny pattern of flowers that was repeated over and over again in the wallpaper. Life was like that, patterns that repeated. She'd tried to change them without looking at the overall picture. "You know, I thought the children needed an image to look up to, to be able to say, 'This is my father.' The more I think about it, really think about it, it's more important that they be proud of themselves."

"Why did you tell me?"

She looked at him—at the man who had finally changed the pattern. How could she explain? She'd found kindness in him where none had been expected. He'd worked beside her though he hadn't been required to. He'd been warm and generous with her children. He had cared for her when she'd been ill. She'd found the kindness beneath the tough exterior, and she had fallen in love with it. With a half sigh, Abby picked up her pen, unconsciously shifting it from hand to hand.

"I can't tell you all the reasons. Once I started talking, it just came, all of it. Maybe I needed to say it out loud now, after all these years. I've never been able to before."

There was a paperweight by her hand, pale pink flowers encased in glass. Fragile to look at, difficult to shatter. "You didn't tell your family?" Dylan asked.

"No. Maybe I should have. You go through all these stages—shame, self-reproach, fury. I needed to work them through."

"Why in God's name did you stay with him?" He thought of the money again, of the woman in mink and diamonds. He no longer wanted to believe that was the reason.

She looked down at her hands. The wedding ring had been gone for a long time, and the bitterness had faded even before that. "After—after it happened, Chuck was devastated. He was miserably sorry. I thought we might salvage something out of that awful night. For a while we nearly did. Then Chris was born. Chuck couldn't look at him without remembering. He'd look at the baby and he'd resent him because of the way he'd come into the world, because Chris reminded him of his own weakness, maybe his own mortality."

"And you? How did you feel when you looked at Chris?"

The smile came slowly. "He was so beautiful. He's still beautiful."

"You're a remarkable woman, Abby."

She looked at him, surprised. "No, I don't think so. I'm a good mother, but there's nothing remarkable about that. I wasn't a good wife. Chuck needed someone who'd pick up and go on a moment's notice. He needed someone who'd race with him. I was too slow."

"What did you need?"

Now she looked at him, her expression blank. No one but her family had ever asked her that. And the pat answers wouldn't come. "I'm not sure what I needed, but I'm happy now with what I have."

"It's enough? The children, this place?" He rose and crossed to her. "I thought you were going to tell me the truth."

"Dylan." He wasn't supposed to be so close. She couldn't think when he stood so close. "I don't know what you expect me to say."

"Don't you?" Taking her hand, he drew her to her feet. He felt her fingers tremble and tightened his grip. "I don't want you to be afraid of me."

"I'm not."

"I don't want you to be afraid of what's between us."

"I can't help it. Dylan, don't do this." She put her free hand on his arm. "I really couldn't stand making a mess of it. I think—I hope we're at the point of being friends."

"We're past that point." He brought her hand to his lips and watched the surprise come into her eyes. "Has anyone ever made love with you?"

Panic sprinted up her spine. "I—I have two children."

"That's not an answer." Curious, he turned her hand over and pressed his lips to the palm. Her fingers curled and tensed. "Was there anyone besides Chuck?"

"No, I—"

His look sharpened, and his fingers tightened. "No one?"

The shame came quickly, the price of failure. "No. I'm really not a physical person."

In how many ways had Rockwell managed to humiliate her? Dylan wondered. Rage came swiftly, and he banked it. Noninvolvement? He was far beyond that now. He wanted to prove to her it could be different. Maybe, for the first time, he wanted to believe it himself.

"Why don't you let me find out for myself?"

"Dylan—" The words clogged in her throat as he brushed his lips over her temple.

"Don't you want me, Abby?" Seduction. He'd never consciously seduced a woman before. Women had always come to him, knowing, experienced, expectant. None of them had ever trembled. He had a moment of panic himself. Did he have it in him to be careful enough, gentle enough, thorough enough?

"Yes." She tilted her head to look at him. "But I don't know what I can give you."

"Let me worry about it." With more confidence than he felt, he took her face in his hands. "For now, just take."

He kissed her slowly, dreamily. Her hands lifted to his wrists and held on. It was that, that hesitant, vulnerable movement, that touched him in a way he'd never expected to be touched. The lamplight fell across her face as he tilted his head and nibbled lightly at her lips. She felt the pulse in his wrists speed up and tightened her hold. He wanted her, really wanted her. And God, she was terrified she'd disappoint both of them. He urged her closer. She stiffened.

"Easy," he murmured, finding patience he hadn't been aware of possessing. "Relax, Abby." He stroked soothingly until he felt her muscles give. Her hands went around his waist, hesitant, tentative. He felt the sweetness of the gesture shoot through him. He'd never looked for sweetness before, never expected it. Now, finding it, he didn't want to lose it.

Slowly, easily, carefully, he made love to her with his mouth alone. Tasting, seducing, then relaxing, he drew her ever so gradually to him. He felt her hands clutch, then loosen at his back. When her mouth warmed and softened against his, he took her deeper. He felt her breath shudder, heard the low, quiet moan that came from wonder. For the first time in years, he felt the wonder himself.

He slipped his hands under her sweater. When she jumped, he stroked and whispered promises he hoped he could keep. Her skin was smooth, her back long and slender. Need whipped through him quickly, painfully. He fought back.

Inch by inch, he brought the sweater up until he could slip it off. It dropped at their feet.

The panic returned. She was vulnerable now. Her breath was coming quickly, somehow clouding her brain. Didn't she have to think? How could she protect herself, how could she give him what he expected if she couldn't think? But his hands felt so wonderful gliding over her skin. Strong, patient, touching her when she needed so badly to be touched. Perhaps when they became demanding she would freeze up, but for now she could only feel the heat building.

Then he led her toward the bed. Fear snapped back into place. "Dylan—"

"Lie down with me, Abby. Just lie down with me."

She held on to him as they lowered to the bed. She saw everything with perfect clarity, the pattern of roses repeated over and over on the walls, the dark spiral of the bedpost, the white square of ceiling. And his face. Nerves tangled and twisted until she was afraid she couldn't move. She struggled with them, trying to remind herself she wasn't a young, inexperienced girl, but a woman.

"The light."

"I want to see you." He kissed her again, eyes open and on hers. "I want you to see me. I'm going to make love to you, Abby. That's nothing that has to be done in the dark."

"Don't—don't expect too much."

He cupped the back of her neck and lifted her face toward his. "Don't expect too little." Then he silenced her.

The kiss sent her spinning. It was hard and pungent. Her body, already tingling with panicked excitement, went hot with passion. The moan ripped out of her and into him. She felt, as she'd once imagined, the scrape of his face against her cheek. Dozens of pulses began to beat in a rhythm that drummed over and over in her head.

She was driving him crazy. Couldn't she feel it? The way her body tensed and shuddered and relaxed, the way her hands reached and hesitated and caressed. He hadn't known he'd wanted her this badly. Not this badly. Now that she was here, warm and solid beneath him, he knew he had to think of her first and his own needs second.

So he showed her. Restlessly, ruthlessly, he stroked his hands over her, feeling her arch, hearing her tangled breaths. He inhaled the passion rising to her skin, that musky, heady, womanly scent a man could drown in. The light slanted over her face so that he could see surprise, pleasure and desire mix and mingle. Impatient, he pulled off his shirt so he could feel his skin against hers.

He was smooth. His torso was hard as iron, but the skin over it was soft. She could glide her fingers over it and feel his muscles tense. Strong. She'd always needed strength, but she'd found it only in herself. Patience. Once she'd nearly wept for patience, but then she'd stopped looking. Now she'd found it. Passion. She'd wanted it, craved it, then dismissed it as something she'd have to live without. Here it was, wrapped around her, burgeoning inside her. He moaned her name, and she was dizzy from the sound of it.

His lips were on her breast. The muscles in her stomach contracted as he encircled the tip with his mouth. Unconsciously she pressed a hand to the back of his head and arched under him. With teeth and tongue and lips he brought her an exquisite torture. Mindlessly she let herself go with it.

He opened the snap of her jeans, but she didn't even notice. She felt the slow movement of his hands, the soft scrape of denim down her legs. She wanted to call out to him, but his name evaporated with a moan as his tongue skimmed over her thigh.

She was beautiful. Her body was slim and subtly muscled, the legs long, the hips narrow. He wondered as he looked at her how she'd ever carried children. Somehow he could only imagine her as untouched. Then he began to see just how high he could take her. And how fast.

The first peak rocked her with uncontrollable speed. Helpless, dazed, Abby gave a muffled cry. It seemed as though her body filled, then burned, then emptied Struggling to right herself, she reached for him, only to have him send her miles higher.

She was gasping for breath, pulsing with sensations she'd never experienced before. Were there names for them? she wondered frantically. Had anyone ever found the right words to describe those feelings? Her skin was so sensitized that even the brush of his fingertip sent her spiraling. He'd wanted to see her like this, floundering in her own pleasure. When he slipped into her, her eyes flew open. He saw the astonished pleasure in them before she reached out to bring him closer.

Her hips moved like lightning, tearing down the control he'd laboriously built. Her fingers dug into his back, the short, rounded nails scraping his skin. She wasn't aware. And soon neither was he.

It had never been like that before. No one had ever made her feel so complete, so important, so alive. Doors had been opened, windows raised, and the air that blew in was wonderful.

She wanted to tell him but was afraid he'd think she was foolish. Instead, she contented herself with placing a hand over his heart. It was beating more steadily than hers, but it was beating very fast.

It had never been like that before. No one had ever made him feel so real, so strong, so open. She'd turned on a light inside his head, and it shone clear and bright. He wanted to tell her but was afraid she'd think he was feeding her a line. Instead, he contented himself with drawing her against him.

"Not very physical, huh?"

"What?"

"You told me you weren't very physical. I guess you didn't want to brag."

She turned her face into his shoulder. Her scent was there, she realized. It was an odd and wonderful sensation to find her own scent clinging to his skin. "I never have been very good at the...at the technical parts."

"Technical parts?" He didn't know whether to laugh or shout at her. "What does that mean?"

"Well, the..." Embarrassed, she let her words trail off. "Sex," she said firmly, reminding herself she was a grown woman.

"We didn't have sex," he said simply, rolling on top of her. "We made love."

"It's just a matter of semantics."

"Like hell it is. No, don't close up on me." He grasped her shoulders hard before she could. "I'm not Chuck. Look at me, really look."

She calmed herself and did what he asked. "I am. I know."

"What do you want, Abby, an evaluation?"

"No." Color flooded cheeks already flushed with passion. "No, of course not. I just—"

"Wonder how it was for me. If you did the right things at the right times." He sat up, pulling her with him, and kept his hands firmly on her shoulders even when she fumbled for the sheet. "Did it ever occur to you that Chuck Rockwell wasn't the devastating macho lover the gossip sheets touted him to be? Did you ever consider that what happened or didn't happen between the two of you in this bed was his fault?"

It hadn't. Of course it hadn't. "All those other women . . ." she began, then fell silent.

"Let me tell you something. It's easy to wrestle under the sheets with a different woman every night." He felt a little twinge, remembering all those times. "You don't have to think, you don't have to feel. You don't have to worry about making the other person see stars. All you do is satisfy yourself. It's very different when you've got a partner, someone you've made promises to, someone you're supposed to want to make happy. It takes care and time and waiting until it's right."

She stared at him, lips parted, eyes wide. With an oath he lifted a hand and ran it through her hair. "Listen, right now I don't much want to hear about Chuck

Rockwell. I don't want you to think about him or anyone else. Just concentrate on me."

"I am." A little uncertain, she touched a hand to his cheek. "You're the best thing that's happened to me in a long time." She saw his expression change, felt his hand tighten in her hair, and went on quickly. "You've made me face a lot of things I thought I should keep under lock and key. I'm grateful."

"I'm getting tired of telling you not to thank me." But his hand gentled in her hair and slipped down to the curve of her shoulder.

"This is absolutely the last time." Lifting her arms, she twined them around him and held tight. She felt safe there, as she'd known she would once before, when the sun had shone down on them. "Don't laugh."

He skimmed his lips over her collarbone. "I don't feel much like laughing."

"I feel as though I've just mastered a very complex and important skill."

He chuckled earning himself a whack on the back. "Like the backstroke?"

"I said not to laugh."

"Sorry." Then he tumbled her over until she lay beneath him. "You don't master anything unless you practice. A lot."

"I guess you're right." This playfulness was something she'd never tasted before. Abby clung to it. Her lips met his, already warm, open and accepting. "Dylan?"

"Hmm?"

"I did see stars."

He smiled. She felt it. When he drew back to look at her, she saw it. "Me, too."

He started to lower his head again, but then he heard the sobbing. ''What the—''

''Chris.'' Abby was out of bed in an instant. She whipped a robe out of her closet, pulled it out and was out of the room before he'd picked up his jeans.

''Oh, baby.'' Abby hurried into Chris's room, where he was bundled under the covers, sobbing his heart out. ''What's the matter?''

''They were green and ugly.'' He burrowed into the safety of his mother's breasts, smelling her familiar smell. ''They looked like snakes and went *Ssss*, and they were chasing me. I fell down in a hole.''

''What a nasty dream.'' She held and rocked and soothed him. ''It's all over now, okay? I'm right here.''

He sniffled but relaxed. ''They were going to cut me up in little pieces.''

''Bad dream?'' Dylan hesitated in the doorway, not certain whether it was his place to come in.

''Ugly green snakes,'' Abby told him as she rocked Chris in her lap.

''Wow. Pretty scary, huh, tiger?''

Chris sniffled again, nodded and rubbed his eyes. Whether it was his place or not, Dylan couldn't resist. He came in and hunkered down in front of the boy. ''Next time you should dream yourself a mongoose. Snakes don't have a chance against a mongoose.''

''Mongoose.'' Chris tried out the word, giggling over it. ''Did you make it up?''

''Nope. We'll find a picture of one tomorrow. They have them in India.''

''Trace went to India,'' Chris remembered. ''We got a postcard.'' Then he yawned and settled back against Abby. ''Don't go yet.''

''No, I won't. I'll stay until you're asleep again.''

"Dylan, too?"

Dylan rubbed his knuckles over the boy's cheek. "Sure."

They sat there, Abby snuggling the boy and singing something that sounded to Dylan like an Irish lullaby. Dylan felt an amazing satisfaction, not like the one he'd found with Abby in the old bed, but one just as strong. It was a firm sense of belonging, as if he had finally reached a place he'd been moving toward all his life. It was foolish, and he told himself it would pass. But it stayed. The hall light slanted into the room and fell on a jumble of trucks next to an old, half-deflated ball.

She settled the boy smoothly, tucking Mary under the sheets with him. Abby kissed his cheek, then straightened, but Dylan stayed for a moment, idly brushing at the curls over Chris's forehead.

"Pretty irresistible, isn't he?" she murmured.

"Yeah." He brought his hand back and stuck it in his pocket. "He's going to be hard to live with when he figures it out."

"He's a lot like Trace—all charm. According to Pop, Trace figured out how to exploit it before he could crawl." In a natural gesture, she took Dylan's hand and drew him out of the room. "I just want to look in on Ben."

She pushed the door open and saw the morass that was her son's room. Clothes, books, toys were one tangled heap that stretched from wall to wall. Abby sighed and promised herself she'd make him see to it over the weekend. At the moment, though, her firstborn was sprawled in bed, half in and half out of the covers.

Going in, she rolled him over, pulled a tennis shoe from under the pillow, tossed aside a squadron of small plastic men and covered him up.

"He sleeps like a rock," she commented.

"So I see."

She took a last look around the room. "He's also a slob."

"Yeah, no argument there."

With a quiet laugh, she bent over and kissed her son. "I love you, you little jerk." She made her way expertly over the heaps in the semidarkness. When she came to the doorway again, Dylan ran his hands down her arms.

"I like your kids, Abby."

Touched, she smiled, then kissed his cheek. "You're a nice man, Dylan."

"There aren't a lot of people who'd agree with you."

She understood that. "Maybe they haven't seen you the way I have."

That much was true, but he couldn't tell her why. He didn't know. "Come back to bed."

She nodded and slipped an arm around his waist.

Chapter Nine

So much could happen in twenty-four hours. Abby faced the morning with a kind of dazed wonder. She'd discovered passion. She'd found affection. And maybe, just maybe, she was taking the first step toward finally severing her ties and obligations to the past. She had Dylan to thank for that, but she didn't think he'd tolerate hearing the phrase again. She couldn't express her gratitude without annoying him. She couldn't tell him that she loved him without risking losing what had just begun. So she would say nothing and hope that simply being with him was enough.

Abby sent the boys off to school, zipped through her morning chores and left a note for Dylan on the breakfast bar, then hopped in her car. She had the energy of ten.

She'd planned to spend the morning mopping, waxing and scrubbing Mrs. Cutterman's house—and earning a good portion of the grocery money. She thought it was a lucky thing she was over the flu and could get back to the part-time job that helped keep the ledgers balanced until she could sell the foals. Tomorrow was also her day to do the twice-monthly cleaning at the Smiths. Mentally she went over her schedule and calculated that she had just enough time to fit everything in, including a shopping expedition for new shoes at the end of the week.

Abby told herself to concentrate on that and not to think too deeply about what had happened the night before. What it had meant to Dylan and what it had meant to her were two different things. She had to be wise enough to understand that. But he'd given her something she'd never had from a man before: respect, affection, passion. She was still relishing it. Switching the radio on, she turned onto the main road.

When Dylan came downstairs, he went straight for the coffee. He didn't usually wake up groggy, even after a sleepless night, but working through the night and lying awake in bed seemed to have different effects. He wasn't sure yet why he'd been so restless. Abby had slept beside him as peacefully as her children had slept in the other rooms.

His body had been relaxed, even serene. He could tell himself that was pure physical relief. But his mind had been tense and active. What had happened between them hadn't been ordinary. Part of him wished it had been, while another—a part he hadn't explored in years—rejoiced that it hadn't. He wasn't a man who enjoyed contrasts within himself. Over and above those contradictions, there was the mystery of the woman who had slept beside him.

He'd begun to dissect the opinion he'd had of her before they'd met and compare it to the feelings he had about her now. Nothing lined up. What did the woman in mink, laughing at the spin of the wheel, have to do with the woman who'd trembled in his arms? Were they both real—or were they both an act?

His blood still curdled when he thought of what she'd told him. For the first time in his life, the urge to protect was stronger than any other. He knew better than to let his feelings color the facts, and he tried to be objective. If she had been physically and emotionally abused, why had she stayed? Chuck Rockwell had publicly thumbed his nose at his wedding vows, so a divorce would have been simple. But she'd stayed. He couldn't resolve the contradiction any more than he could resolve what was happening inside him.

He wanted her, just as much as he had before—no, even more. There was a sweetness about her lovemaking that he'd never tasted before, and he craved it again. But there was more. He could close his eyes and hear the way she laughed at herself, easily and without guile. He could see the way she worked, steadily and without bitterness. There was the way she handled her children, with a firm hand and tremendous love.

A special woman. He knew only a fool believed there was anything as fanciful as a special woman. Maybe he was becoming a fool.

He glanced out the window and wondered if she was in the barn feeding the stock. He could wait for her to come in again, have his recorder ready, and they'd get down to work. Dylan pictured her hefting a bag of grain or hefting another bale of hay. With a shake of his head, he turned and reached for his coat. Then he saw the note.

> Dylan
> I'm at Mrs. Cutterman's through the morning. The number is in the book if there's a problem. I need to swing into town and pick up a few things before I come home. See you around one.
>   Abby

He felt ridiculously depressed. She wasn't there, wouldn't be there for hours. He wanted to see her, to look at her in the morning, see her face after their night together. He wanted to talk to her, calmly, logically, until what he knew and what he felt drew closer together. He wanted to make love with her in the daylight in the big, empty house.

He wanted to be with her.

Shrugging off the feeling, Dylan poured a second cup of coffee and took it upstairs. There was work to be done.

When Abby pulled up in front of the house, the sky had darkened again. She muttered halfheartedly at the clouds as she carried the bread and milk to the house. Rain, she thought, disgusted because the radio had promised clear skies. Neither of the boys had their boots with them. Well, they needed new shoes anyway, she reminded herself, and pushed open the door. On her way to the kitchen, she picked up two trucks, two plastic men and a sock.

After shedding her coat, she switched on the portable radio and began to deal with the ground beef she'd taken out to defrost that morning.

"Hi."

She jumped a little, a frying pan in one hand. Dylan was only two feet away. "Lord, you're quiet. I didn't hear you come in."

"You always play the radio too loud."

"Oh." Automatically she lowered the volume. She felt awkward, but she'd expected to. "I had to pick up some milk. The way the boys go through it, I'm tempted to buy a cow." She busied herself at the stove and felt a little easier. "You've been working?"

"Yeah." He felt awkward. He hadn't expected it. Soft and straight, her hair was tied back with a bandanna. He wanted to loosen it, to feel it flow through his hands the way it had during the night. "Did you have a good time?"

"What?"

"A good time." The meat began to sizzle. "With your friend."

"My—oh, Mrs. Cutterman. She's very nice." Abby thought briefly of the acres of furniture she'd polished. Dismissing the thought, she began to rummage for tomato paste. "It's going to rain," she said. "I don't think the boys are going to make it home before it does."

"You had a call."

"Oh?"

"Betty something from the PTA."

"Bake sale." With a sigh, Abby opened the can of tomato paste. The whirl of the electric can opener sounded like an earthquake. How long, she wondered, could she hide behind routine? "Cupcakes?"

"Three dozen. She said she knew she could count on you."

"Good old reliable Abby." She said it without sarcasm, but with a self-mocking tone. "When does she need them?"

"Next Wednesday."

"Okay." The silence went on as she diluted the paste and added spices. Spaghetti was Ben's favorite, she thought. He packed it away like a lumberjack. At the moment, she didn't know if she would ever eat again. "I guess you'd like to ask me more questions."

"A few."

"I'll be finished here in a minute. If we can do it while I'm seeing to the laundry, then..." Her voice trailed off when he touched her shoulder. No longer knowing what to expect, she turned slowly. He was looking at her again, looking deep, looking hard. She wished she understood what he was searching for.

Then he kissed her, softly, gently, and her heart melted like butter.

"Oh, Dylan." The breath she hadn't been aware of holding escaped unevenly as she put her arms around him. "I was afraid you had regrets."

"About what?" God, it felt good to hold her. He'd told himself it made no difference, but it did. It made all the difference.

"About last night."

"No, I have no regrets." She smelled of soap—just as fresh as that. "I'm dazed."

"Really?" Only half believing him, she drew back.

"Yeah, really." He smiled, incredibly relieved, and kissed her again. "I missed you."

"Oh, that's nice." She ran her hands up his back as she drew him closer. "That's very nice."

"Want to play hooky?"

With a laugh, she tossed back her head. "Hooky?"

"That's right. You look like someone who never played enough hooky."

"I was never in one school long enough to work up to it. Besides, it's going to rain. What kind of fun is it to play hooky in the rain?"

"Come upstairs, I'll show you."

She laughed again, but her eyes widened when she saw he was serious. "Dylan, the kids'll be home in a couple of hours."

"You can pack a whole day into a couple of hours." On impulse, he scooped her up. It felt good, he realized, to hear that quick, breathless laugh, to see those wide, wondering eyes.

Her heart pounded as he carried her from the room. It was thrilling, illicit. Abby buried her face against his throat and murmured. "No one's going to have any clean socks."

"And only you and I will know why."

They made love quickly, desperately, with a wild kind of abandon she'd never experienced before. Clothes were tossed helter-skelter around the room. The curtains were thrown wide so that the soft, gloomy light crept into the room. He took her places she'd never been, places she knew she'd be afraid to go with anyone else. Like a child treated to her first roller coaster, she lost her breath on the ride, then fretted to go again.

He felt free, so incredibly free, as they rolled over on the old bed. Her body was furnace-hot and open to him, open to anything he could teach her. She was pliant, she was strong. And she was his. Amazingly agile, she arched back, lost in mindless pleasure. Unable to get enough, he rose with her. Their bodies met, torso to torso, hip to hip, as they knelt on the bed. Tight as bowstrings, then limp, they tumbled together.

It began to rain, slow and steady against the windows.

Their loving slowed and steadied as passion turned to yearning. Quiet sighs, gentle movements took the place of frenzy. There was no need to rush. The bed was wide and soft, the rain quiet and soothing. They drew from each other all the sweet, simple things lovers bring to one another and no one else.

He tasted her skin, warm with pleasure, damp with excitement. He'd never known a flavor more intoxicating. Her fingers trailed over his back, finding the muscles that contracted and gave. She'd never known strength in itself could be so arousing.

They went deep into each other where the rain could no longer be heard. She found what she'd needed to find—the kindness, the compassion.

There were so many layers to her—serenity, wisdom, passion. He wondered if he would ever discover them all. He could look at her one way and see the headstrong woman who'd thrown caution to the winds and left family and familiar things to grab at something as elusive as love. He could look at her another way and see the vulnerability and the control. He felt compelled to know her, to fit the pieces together. Abby was becoming his obsession. But when they were like this, desire peaking, senses swimming, it only mattered that she was there with him.

The hands that had once been hesitant moved over him as though they'd always known him. The mouth that had once been unsure fused to his as though there were no other tastes in the world she would ever need. Her long, limber body came to his without inhibitions.

Her arms and legs wrapped around him like warm silk. Passion poured through them, swirled around them, until there was nothing else.

Abby was walking downstairs, delighted with herself, when the front door burst open. "Wipe your feet," she said automatically, then laughed and hurried down the rest of the stairs to hug her two dripping children.

"It's raining," Chris informed her.

"Really?"

"My papers got wet." Ben took off his soaking hat and let it fall on the floor.

"They wouldn't if you used your book bag."

"They're for girls." He picked up his hat because his mother was looking at it, then handed her a wet, wrinkled paper.

"An A!" Abby put a hand to her heart as if the shock were too much for her. "Why, Benjamin, someone put your name on their paper."

He chuckled, a bit embarrassed. "No, they didn't. It's mine."

"This spelling test—unit 31—with none, absolutely none, marked wrong, belongs to Benjamin Francis Rockwell? My Benjamin Francis Rockwell?"

He wrinkled his nose as he always did when reminded of his middle name. "Yeah."

She put a hand on his shoulder. "You know what this means?" she asked solemnly.

"What?"

"Hot chocolate all around."

A grin split his face. "Can I have marshmallows?"

"Absolutely."

"Hot chocolate?" Dylan asked as he came down the steps.

Abby hooked an arm around Ben's shoulder. "We're celebrating the one hundred percent, grade A, unit 31. Twenty death-defying words spelled correctly." She held up the paper where the little gold star glittered damply.

"Pretty impressive." Dylan scrubbed a hand over Chris's head, then held it out to Ben. "Congratulations."

"It's no big deal," he murmured, but looked secretly pleased with the handshake. "Can I have three marshmallows?"

"The boy knows how to take advantage of a situation," Abby stated. "Let's go. Hang up your coats," she said automatically when they stepped into the kitchen.

For the next twenty minutes, the air was filled with stories of the adventures young boys go through in a day. Then bloated with chocolate, Ben and Chris tugged on their boots and coats and went out to tend the stock.

"I bet I haven't had any of this for twenty years," Dylan mused as he studied his empty cup.

"Bring back memories?"

"My mother used to make it." When Abby leaned on the counter opposite him and smiled, he found himself continuing. "She's a great cook. I still think she bakes the best custard pies in New Jersey."

"Do you get to see them often? Your parents?"

"Couple of times a year." He shrugged, feeling the familiar tug of guilt and resignation. "There never seems to be enough time."

"I know." Abby glanced over her shoulder at the window. There would come a time when her boys would go, when she'd have to let them go. That was the price of being a parent. "I don't see mine very often, either. They're never in one place long enough."

"Still playing the clubs?"

"They'll always be playing the clubs." Affection came into her voice, deep and natural. "Put two people into a room and they're ready to entertain. It's in the blood, if you believe my father's theory. He's desperately proud of Chantel and Maddy for carrying on the tradition in grand style. He stays annoyed with Trace because he didn't."

"What does your brother do?"

"Travels." She moved her shoulders. "None of us really have any idea just what it is that Trace does." She took another cookie off the plate and offered Dylan one. "Pop claims Trace doesn't know, either."

"What about you? Any problems because you don't sing for your supper?"

"Oh, no." She grinned. "I gave them Ben and Chris—better than a command performance. Your parents must be proud of you."

"My father would have preferred it if I'd stayed on the farm and milked cows." He drew out a cigarette. "But my mother tells me he's read every word I've written."

"Isn't if funny how—"

"Mom!" Chris came barreling through the door, dripping wet and tracking mud. Abby caught him halfway into the room, checking for injuries.

"What is it? What's wrong?"

"It's Eve. She's sick. She's lying down and all sweaty."

Abby already had her coat off the hook. Not bothering to change into her boots, she dashed out the door in her sneakers. When she got to the barn, Ben was sitting next to the mare, struggling not to cry as he stroked her.

"Is she going to die?"

Abby crouched beside him and put a hand on the mound of the mare's stomach. "No, no, of course not." She circled her arm around Ben and squeezed hard. "She's just going to have a baby. Remember, we talked about it."

"She looks awful sick."

"When babies come, it hurts some. But she's going to be fine." With her heart in her throat, Abby prayed she wasn't making promises she couldn't keep. "She's having contractions," she murmured, soothing the mare. "Her body's helping the baby come out."

All Ben could see was the mare's shudders. Sweat rolled, dampening her coat and overwhelming the scent of fresh hay. "Why does it have to hurt?"

"Because life hurts a little, Ben. But it's worth it." One of the barn cats mewed in sympathy as Eve moaned. "Now, Ben, I want you to go in and call the vet. Tell him who you are first, okay?"

He sniffed. "'Kay."

"Then tell him that Eve's in labor."

"In labor?"

"Having a baby's work," she told him, and kissed his cheek. "Go ahead. Then come back. This is something you'll want to see."

He dashed off, recovered enough to be pleased with the responsibility. As the mare suffered her pangs, Abby shifted Eve's head onto her lap.

"Anything we can do?"

She looked up to see Dylan standing at the entrance to the stall, Chris's hand firmly caught in his. Her son was wide-eyed and fascinated. She smiled.

"I've helped the vet with deliveries before, and I found that you end up doing little more than cheering her on. Eve has the starring role here." Eve moaned with the next contraction, and Abby leaned over and crooned to her. "Oh, I know it hurts, baby." The mare's sweat transferred to her own skin. Abby wished she could take some of the pain as easily.

Chris swallowed with a little click. He'd never seen anything like it. One of the cats had had kittens once, he remembered. But he'd come out to the barn to find them snuggled, clean and naked, against their mother. "Did it hurt when I was born?"

"You were a slowpoke." The mare's eyes half shut, and she breathed heavily. With her hand on Eve's stomach, Abby felt the power of the contraction. "For a while I thought you'd decided not to come out after all. The doctor had music on. They were playing 'Let It Be' when you were born."

"Would Eve like the music?"

"I bet she would."

Anxious to help, Chris dashed over and turned on the radio. A familiar ballad filled the air.

"The vet said he'd come as soon as he could but not to worry 'cause Eve's real strong." Ben dashed back in and took his place beside his brother.

"Of course she is."

But as the minutes dragged on and the contractions built, Abby worried. She knew she could handle a simple foaling, with or without the vet. When a woman lived on her own, raised children on her own, she had no choice but to develop self-confidence. But if there were complications... She shook her head and cleared her mind. Whatever happened, she was going to give Eve the best she could. The horse meant more, much more, than a means to an end to her. Eve was flesh and blood, something she'd cared for day after day for over a year. When pain went through the mare, it rippled through her. Then Dylan crouched beside her.

"She's doing fine," he assured her. "Look, I never delivered any horses, but I helped with my share of cows."

She leaned her head on his shoulder briefly in a gesture that caught Ben's attention. "Thanks."

But when it began, Abby rushed to help the foal into the world before Dylan could. Her own sweat mixed with the mare's, and her voice was raised in encouragement. The blood that came with new life streaked her hands. The hope that came with new life shone in her eyes. She looked, Dylan realized as he watched her, magnificent. He glanced at the boys and saw them watching the foal's birth with their mouths hanging open.

"Incredible, isn't it?"

Ben looked at him and made a face. "It's pretty gross." Then he saw spindly legs emerge, a small head and a compact body. "It's a horse. It's a real horse." Both he and Chris scrambled for a closer look.

"But he's big." Intrigued, Chris measured the foal. "How'd he fit in there?"

"She," Abby corrected, weeping shamelessly. "Isn't she beautiful?"

"She's kind of sloppy," Ben commented. Then Eve immediately went about her business and cleaned up her baby.

"Good job." Dylan stroked a hand down Abby's hair, then kissed her. "Real good job."

Chris reached out a tentative hand to touch the foal. "Can we play with her?"

"Not yet ... but you can touch. Isn't she soft?"

Then Chris jerked back as the foal shook and shivered and tried out her legs for the first time. "She stood up!" Amazed, he stared at his mother. "She stood right up. Cathy Jackson's little sister didn't stand up for months and months." It pleased him enormously to find his horse superior. "What can we name her?"

"We can't name her, love. If Mr. Jorgensen's going to buy her, then he'll want to name her."

"We can't keep her?"

"Chris ..." She looked at him and at Ben. "You know we can't. We talked about this."

"You didn't sell Ben and me."

"Horses grow up faster," Dylan put in. "One day you'll have a house of your own. The foal's going to be ready for her own place in a few months."

"We can visit her." Ben set his chin and waited for someone to shoot him down.

"I'm sure we can." Abby smiled at him. Her baby was so grown-up already. "Mr. Jorgensen's a very nice man."

"Can we watch when Gladys has her baby?" Ben reached out for the first time to touch the foal's ears.

"If you're not in school." She heard the sound of an engine and looked down at her hands. For the first time, she noticed they were streaked with blood. "That must be the vet. I'd better wash."

The excitement didn't die down until long after bedtime. Because she understood, Abby let her boys go out and say good-night to the foal after they should both have been in bed themselves. Tired, but pleasantly so, she settled down in front of the living room fire.

"Quite a day," Dylan murmured as he sat beside her.

"And then some. I'm so glad the boys were there. It's something they'll never forget. It's something I'll never forget." She felt a stirring inside her, one she hadn't experienced for a long, long time. She knew what it was like to have life grow inside her, what it was like to bring it into a not-so-perfect world. Would she ever carry another child? She sighed, reminding herself she had two beautiful healthy sons.

"Tired?"

"A little."

"Your mind's wandering."

She curled her legs under her and watched the flames dance. "I think you see too much in there too easily."

"Funny, I would have said I haven't seen nearly enough."

She blocked off wishes and longings and faced reality. "Tomorrow you're going to have more questions, and you're going to expect me to answer them."

"That's what I'm here for, Abby." But he wasn't sure that was the complete truth, not now.

"I know." She accepted it as truth. She had to. "I've made myself a few promises, Dylan. I'm going to try to keep them."

He touched her hair, wishing there were other ways to get what he needed to get from her. "There aren't any questions right now."

She closed her eyes a moment. Maybe there was a little room for longings after all. "For tonight, just for tonight, I'd like to pretend there isn't any book, that there aren't any questions."

He knew he could have pressed. He understood that at that moment she was open enough to tell him everything. If he pushed the right buttons, the answers would simply pour out. He had an obligation to do it. He slipped an arm around her shoulder and watched the fire with her.

"We had a big stone fireplace at home. My mother used to say you could roast an ox in it."

She relaxed against him as if it were the most natural thing in the world. "Were you happy?"

"Yeah. I never much cared for milking cows before the sun came up, but I was happy. We had a creek and a big oak tree. I'd sit under it, listen to the water and read books. I could go anywhere."

She smiled, picturing him as a child. "And you decided to be a writer."

"I decided to single-handedly spread the truth. I guess that's why reporting came first. I went into that with the First Amendment playing in my head." He laughed at himself, something he didn't yet realized he'd learned from her. "I found out you've got to crawl through a lot of dirt to make it work."

"The truth." She closed her eyes and wished the word didn't have such a sharp edge. "It's very important to you."

"Without it the rest is just dressing, just excuses."

She'd made plenty of those, Abby thought. "Why biographies, then?"

"Because it's fascinating to explore one person's life, one person at a time, and find out how many other lives were affected, what marks were left, what mistakes were made."

"Sometimes mistakes are private."

"That's why I've never done a bio that wasn't authorized."

"And if one day someone wrote yours?"

He seemed to find that amusing. She heard his chuckle as his cheek brushed over her hair. He couldn't know how deadly serious she was. "Maybe I'd do it myself—warts and all."

"Have you ever done anything you were really ashamed of?"

He didn't have to think for long. A man didn't live beyond thirty without shame. "I've had my share of wrong turns."

"And you'd write about them, no matter what anyone thought of you after it was done?"

"You can't bargain with the truth, Abby." He remembered what she had told him about Chris's conception and continued, "Sometimes, when it's important enough, you can pretend you didn't hear it."

She watched the fire and thought about that. She thought about it a long time.

Because he wanted to get an early start, Dylan was downstairs before the boys had finished breakfast. The main topic, as expected, was the foal. The boys were arguing, though without heat, about whether Gladys would mess things up and deliver while they were in school. Veterans now, they were prepared to step in as midwives. To prove their valor, each one had a Polaroid snapshot of the new addition to take to class.

"They're having hamburgers for lunch today," Ben remembered, looking expectantly at his mother.

Abby put the jar of peanut butter back in the cupboard. "Get my purse."

"Me, too?" Chris asked dribbling milk down his chin.

"Okay." She opened her bag when Ben brought it in, and dumped out the contents. Along with her wallet, she pulled a pair of rubber gloves in a plastic bag out of the pile and dropped them on the counter. "Here you go. Don't lose it."

"We won't." Chris scrambled for his coat while he stuffed the money in the pocket of his jeans. "Mom, I know where babies come from."

"Um-hmm." She was pouring her second cup of coffee.

"But how do they get there?"

"Oh." She spilled the coffee on the counter, and caught Dylan's grin as she turned to look at Chris. His round young face was lifted to hers. But he's only six, she thought, wondering just what she was supposed to tell him. She knelt down in front of him and asked herself how to tell a six-year-old about making babies in the two minutes he had left before he had to catch the bus for school.

"Love puts them there," she told him, and kissed both his cheeks. "A very special kind of love."

"Oh." Satisfied, he gave her one of his quick, energetic hugs and dashed for the door. "Come on, Ben." Then, seeing that his brother was still pulling on his coat, Chris grinned. "I'll beat you." He flew off with the challenge and left Ben struggling to zip up and run at the same time.

"Bye, Ben," Abby murmured. Then, with a shake of her head, she went back to mop up the coffee.

Dylan sat at the counter and watched her tidy up the spill with a secret smile of amusement on her face. "I like your style, lady."

"Oh?" Laughing, she tugged at the hem of an over-laundered sweatshirt. "It is rather *today* isn't it?"

"I was talking about your answer to a very important and very ticklish question from a six-year-old boy. Some people would've given him a biology lesson, and others would have brushed him off. You gave him exactly the answer he needed. Still . . ." He toyed with the last of his coffee. "I wish I'd had that Polaroid when the question popped out of his mouth. Your face was worth the price of a ticket."

"I'm sure it was." She walked over to pull on her boots.

"I like the way you look in the morning."

She stopped, still bent over, and looked at him. "Frazzled?"

"Fresh." The smile on her face faded. "Soft." His voice lowered. "I'd like to be able to lie in bed with you during the morning, watch you wake up, fall back to sleep and know when you wake up again I could make love with you."

Her pulse thudded, and she wondered he didn't hear it. "I'd like that, too. But the children—"

"I didn't say I didn't understand. But the idea warms me up a little."

It warmed her more than a little, she thought as she finally managed to get into her boots. "As it is, there isn't a lot of time around here for lazing around in bed in the morning. I always figure I'll know the kids are growing up when they sleep past seven." Not quite steady, she walked over to clear the counter.

"I'll do that," he said, and caught her hand.

"It's all right."

"Abby . . ." He flicked a finger over her wrist. "Haven't you ever heard of women's liberation?"

She lifted a brow. In her way, she'd been liberated since she'd taken her first breath. Her parents had seen to that. "Sure. That's why the boys take turns doing the dishes, put away their own clothes—on a good day—

and know how to use the vacuum. Their wives will thank me. In the meantime, someone has to man the oars."

"There are usually two oars."

She tilted her head, smiled, then nodded. "Fine. You clean up the kitchen, I'll feed the stock. It'll save some time."

"Okay. We'll get started when you come back in."

"Can't." She started to clear the contents of her purse from the counter. "I have to run over to the Smiths' this morning. I'll be back around noon."

He started to object, then made himself stop. She had her own life. He watched her fill her purse again. "Do you always carry rubber gloves in there?"

"What? Oh." With a laugh, she dropped them in. "I do when I'm going to the Smiths'. She's a fanatic about ammonia."

"Come again?"

"Ammonia." Abby zipped up her purse and wondered if there was enough spaghetti in the fridge for leftovers. "The straight stuff. The woman has a fetish about having all the floors cleaned with ammonia."

His brow creased as he tried to follow her. "You clean them?"

"Twice a month." Her mind on dozens of other matters, Abby went for her coat.

"What is it, like volunteer work?"

She have a quick, appreciative roll of laughter as she turned back. "Not on your life. I make six dollars an hour. Look, don't run the dishwasher. I think—"

"You work as a maid?"

"Housekeeper." She grinned and pulled a bandanna off a peg to tie her hair back with. "I suppose that's really a glorified term, but I always see a maid in a little black skirt, and..." She let the words die when he rose out of his seat and walked to her. Something in his eyes had her throat clogging up. She'd never dealt well with anger.

"Why in the hell are you getting down on your hands and knees and scrubbing someone else's floor?"

Her chin came up. "It's honest work."

"Why?"

"Because the only other thing I'm good at is singing in three-part harmony. There isn't a lot of call for that, and the pay's lousy."

Ignoring her evasions, he went straight to the point. "Why does Chuck Rockwell's widow have to wash floors for six dollars an hour?"

She went very pale. It was in his voice, the doubt, the derision. "I don't have time or the inclination to discuss my financial business with you, Dylan." She yanked the door open, but he slammed it again.

"I asked you a question."

"And I've given you the only answer I intend to." The fire came into her eyes, briefly but powerfully. "I don't have to tolerate this from you, from anyone, Dylan. I don't have to stand here while you look at me as though I'm less of a person because I mop other people's floors and dust their furniture for pay. If I did it for charity I'd be a hero, but I do it for money."

"I want to know why you do it at all."

"I do exactly what I have to do. Nobody knows it better."

With that she yanked the door open again and strode out. He could have followed her, and he started to.

Then, just as determined as she, Dylan shut the door. It was time to get back to business, he told himself. And back to the truth.

Chapter Ten

Moving with a dull, grinding fury, Dylan drafted out twenty pages. Chuck Rockwell had become more than a name, less than an image to him now. Over the course of time, Dylan had come to know him as a man, a badly flawed one, insecure, self-absorbed, intemperate. The skill and the training couldn't be overlooked, nor could the daring that some would have called heroics. He'd been born not just with a silver spoon in his mouth, but with the whole place setting at his disposal. Yet he hadn't chosen to simply sit back and enjoy his wealth, he'd refused a meaningless title in the family conglomerate. He had, instead, chosen to make his own mark in his own way. There was something to be said for that.

Chuck Rockwell had become a success and had earned respect, even adulation. His associates had considered him one of their best, even if they hadn't liked him personally. The press had gloried in him, on the track and off. His fans had made him a celebrity within a year of his first professional race. He'd attained all that, plus a devoted wife and two sons.

Then he'd set out—systematically, it seemed to Dylan—to destroy it all.

He'd lost his backer and first supporter, he'd alienated most of his associates and had torn irreparable holes in his marriage. Yet Abby had once described him as a knight on a white charger. And she'd stuck by him for four years.

Why?

Chuck had abused their marriage, abused her and left her to raise his children while he ran the next race and pursued the next woman. But she'd made a home for him.

Why?

Until she told him, until he cornered her again and pulled the answers out of her, what he wrote would just be words.

Until she told him, until she trusted him with the truth, what he felt for her couldn't be acknowledged.

How long could he deny it? Dylan crushed his cigarette out with quick and deliberate violence. How long could he live in the same house with her, watch her, want her, deny he'd lost his head over her? Lost his head. With self-mocking laugh, he ran his hands over his face. It was easier to plead insanity than to admit he'd lost his heart. What he'd done was fall in love.

But he'd always thought that falling in love meant you'd stumbled, slipped, that you hadn't looked for the rocks in the road or noticed the edge of the cliff. And he'd been right. He felt as if he'd slipped, stumbled and caught himself on one of those rocks, then taken a nosedive off the cliff. In all likelihood, it was going to screw up his book, his objectivity and his life.

He wished to God she would come home.

That was another problem, he admitted. He'd been on the farm less than three weeks and he already thought of it as home. He'd been with Abby less than three weeks and he already thought of her as his. And the boys... Dylan pushed away from his desk and strode around the room. All right, so he was crazy about them. He wasn't made of stone, was he?

It didn't have to make any difference. He'd worked too hard to get his life exactly the way he wanted it. The only person he was responsible to was himself, the only person he had to satisfy was himself. The only person who had to approve of him was Dylan Crosby.

Maybe he wasn't rolling in money, but he certainly made enough. If he wanted to take off tomorrow for three weeks in the South Seas, there was no one he'd have to clear it with first. Selfish? Dylan turned that over in his mind with a shrug. What if he were? He was entitled. He'd milked cows until the time he'd gone to college. He'd studied hard, worked hard, and had established himself professionally and personally. His years as an investigative reporter had been fiendish in their way, but he'd gotten through them. His marriage hadn't exactly been made in heaven, but he'd done the best he could with it while it had lasted. Now he was free, with no ties, no strings. He set his own schedules, made his own demands. Just because he liked the farm and was fond of a couple of kids didn't mean he was going to turn his world upside down. He'd been through one marriage, and so had Abby. They'd be smart not to step back into the ring.

When was she coming home?

The minute he heard the engine, he was at the window. But it wasn't Abby's sturdy station wagon that pulled up. It was a huge gunmetal-gray limo.

"Ah, fresh air. Country air." Frank O'Hurley bounced out of the limo as though it were act one, scene one. "Clears the mind. Cleanses the soul. Everybody should breathe it in." He did, then screwed up his face. "God save us. What is that smell?"

"Horse manure'd be my guess." Maddy stepped out beside him, then looked around with quick, avid curiosity. Fifty-second Street or Dogpatch, it made no difference to her. "Mom, did I leave my purse in there?"

"Right here." Molly, slim and pretty, accepted the driver's hand before stepping out. She stood on sturdy legs and shaded her eyes against the sun. Sunlight made wrinkles. She wasn't particularly vain, but her face was part of her act. "Ah." With a look that was half pleased, half baffled, she stared at the house. "Such a place. I can never quite imagine our Abby here."

"Where'd we go wrong?" Frank asked her, and got a quick swipe on the shoulder from his youngest daughter.

"Cut it out, Pop. Abby loves this place."

Dylan came to the door just in time to see Chantel O'Hurley step from the limo onto the sparsely graveled drive. It struck him first that Abby had the same million-dollar legs as Chantel. He watched as her skirt flared beautifully around her and she took the driver's hand, then flashed a smile designed to turn a man to putty.

"Thank you, Donald." Her voice was like smoke and seemed to encircle her listeners sensuously. "If you'd just put our bags on the porch, that will be all for today."

"Very good, Miss O'Hurley."

"You do that so well," Maddy murmured as the driver popped the hood.

"Darling, I was born to do it." Then, as she laughed and linked her arm through her sister's, she spotted Dylan. "Well, well." It might have been a purr, but kittens didn't purr when they showed their teeth. "What have we here?"

"Must be the writer." Maddy gave him a brief and thorough summing-up. "Be nice."

"Maddy, remember my image." Chantel slid her oversize sunglasses down her nose and continued to stare. "Nice had nothing to do with it."

As the two women paused, Dylan did some summing-up of his own. One sister was dressed in baggy slacks and an oversize jacket whose contrasting shades of green and blue should have hurt the eyes. Instead, the pattern was as bright and cheerful as her short mop of strawberry-blond hair. Beside her was the image of cool, understated glamour, from the long silvery-blond mane to the toes of her alligator pumps. Standing next to them were a small, pretty woman of about fifty and a wiry little man making theatrical gestures toward the barn.

Maddy was the first to step forward. "Hello, we're Abby's family."

She walked up the steps with the quick, swinging gait of a born optimist. Her sister followed with the slow, alluring moves of a born siren. "Dylan Crosby." Chantel extended the tips of her fingers. "We've met."

"Miss O'Hurley." If he'd ever seen a woman who'd have liked to ram a knife into him—and one who would have known precisely the right spot to aim for—it was this one. Dylan turned to Maddy.

"You're the writer." She sent her sister an amused, knowing glance. "Abby told us you'd be here. These are our parents."

"Frank and Molly O'Hurley." Frank stuck his hand out and shook with fast, friendly exuberance.

"Molly and Frank," his wife said with a smile. Dylan could see where Abby had inherited her looks.

"Always worried about billing." Frank pecked his wife's cheek before turning back to Dylan. "Where's my girl?"

"Abby had to run some errands." Dylan was a man who believed in first impressions, and he was immediately drawn to the small, spry man with the big grin and the well-timbred voice.

"Errands." Frank slipped an arm around his wife and gave her a squeeze. "Just like our Abby."

"And totally unlike the rest of us. Hello." Molly didn't offer her hand, but smiled at Dylan. "You must be the writer. Abby told us she'd decided to authorize the book."

"That's right." She didn't have to say any more to convey her disapproval. Yet Dylan felt it was directed at the project rather than himself. It wasn't everyone who could make such a fine distinction felt so easily. "I don't know exactly when she'll be back, but—"

"No problem." Frank gave him a companionable pat on the arm, then strode past him into the house. The move was so smooth, so natural, that it took Dylan a minute to realize Frank had ignored the pile of luggage. Maddy hauled up two bags and sent Dylan a wink.

"Pretty sharp, isn't he? Come on, Chantel, just like old times."

Chantel cast a long, considering look at the pile, paused, then chose one small leather tote.

"Takes after her father," Molly commented as she leaned over to grasp the handle of a suitcase.

"I'll take care of it," Dylan began, but Molly laughed and hefted the bag herself.

"I've been lugging trunks since I could stand. Don't worry about me, you'll have your hands full with the rest, because I can promise you they won't be back for them. Put on some coffee, Frank," she called out, then walked up the staircase without a backward glance.

With a shrug, Dylan stacked and lifted the remaining bags and followed. It looked as if it might be an interesting afternoon.

Abby decided there was little purpose in nursing her temper. Perhaps it was justified, perhaps in its way it was satisfying. But it just didn't accomplish anything. Dylan didn't trust her. If she was honest, she had to admit he had no real reason to. While she could rationalize that she hadn't lied to him, neither had she been completely honest. Dylan Crosby was a man who required the unvarnished truth.

He'd hurt her. His doubts and derision had hurt her. She had wanted to believe they'd reached some point of understanding. She'd hoped they'd come far enough in their relationship for him to accept her for who and what she was.

She had wanted too much. The trouble was, Abby longed for more. She wanted his trust, though she hadn't been able to give her own. She wanted his support, though she was afraid to offer hers. She wanted his love most of all, yet she wouldn't admit her own feelings for him.

Temper had given her a smug sense of self-satisfaction, but only temporarily. It had also left her unsettled and unhappy. Maybe the time had come for her to put her feelings on the line and give Dylan what seemed most important to him. Complete honesty. If she opened up and he still walked away from her, she could have no regrets.

When Abby pulled up in the drive, she had decided to tell Dylan everything—the mistakes, the regrets, the compromises. Without faith, love was just another word. She would put her life in his hands and believe in him.

The minute she opened the front door, her nerve started to weaken. She had to talk to him and talk to him quickly, before she pulled back. Then she saw him coming from the direction of the kitchen. Abby stood where she was and waited for her resolve to harden. "Dylan." She shifted her bag from hand to hand. "We need to talk."

"Yeah." He'd made his own decisions that morning. "It might have to wait a little while."

"It can't. I—" Abby caught a movement out of the corner of her eye and turned toward the stairs. Maddy stood there, barefoot, her hands deep in the pockets of baggy slacks. She grinned as though she knew every secret in the world and was ready to tell them.

"Maddy!" Before the name was fully formed, Abby rushed toward the staircase and threw herself into her sister's arms. First came laughter; then they both began to talk at once. Somehow, in the torrent of words, they both managed to ask and answer a half a dozen questions.

"You two always stepped on each other's lines." From the top of the staircase, Chantel looked down.

Dylan noted that she looked just as cool, just as elegant, as she had when she'd stepped from the limo. Then, with a whoop, she was clattering down the stairs at a dangerous speed to launch herself at her sisters.

"Both of you." Abby had an arm around each sister, holding them close. One smelled free, easy, fresh, the other dark and tempting. "How did you manage it?"

"I backed out of the play." Maddy said with a laugh. She hadn't realized until it was done, how badly she'd needed to move on. "My understudy is building a shrine to me."

"We shot the final scenes of the movie last week." Chantel gave a lazy shrug. "I left my leading man desolate." Then she stepped back, taking Abby's face in her hand. She turned it one way, then the other, her eyes narrowed. "Incredible," she muttered. "Not a bit of makeup. That's why I hate you."

Abby hugged them both again. "Oh, God, I'm so glad to see you."

There was a hint, only a hint, of desperation in her voice. It was enough. Over Abby's head, Chantel aimed a long, hard look at Dylan. Her eyes were blue, a very dark, very intense blue. She knew how to use them.

Sensitive to changes in mood, Maddy felt the tension. The best way to deal with it, in her opinion, was to slide over it. "I hate to use old lines," she said easily, "but you ain't seen nothin' yet. Come into the kitchen. How about some coffee, Dylan?"

Her look was so friendly that he wondered if he imagined the message beneath. Her eyes weren't the vivid blue of Chantel's or the deep green of Abby's. They were a warm shade of brandy uniquely her own.

But the challenge was there. Acknowledging it, he walked in to the kitchen with them.

"Mom. Pop." Stunned, Abby stared at her parents, who were sitting cozily at the breakfast bar.

"It's about time you got home, girl." Frank swiveled in his chair and grinned at her. His arms opened in the wide, inviting gesture that had always warmed her. "Let's have a kiss."

"What are you doing here?" She had an arm around each parent, drawing in the old, familiar scents—peppermint and Chanel. Her father couldn't get through a day without peppermints, and her mother would go without shoes before she denied herself her perfume. "There isn't a theater within twenty miles."

"Vacation." Her father have her another smacking kiss. "It was either here or Paris."

Molly gave a quick, none-too-subtle snort, then picked up her coffee. "Where are the boys?"

"In school. They'll be home a bit after three."

"All day stuck with books." Frank shook his head. "It's a tragedy."

"Just keep that to yourself," Abby warned. "They'll be too glad to agree with you."

"What's this?" Frank reached up and brushed a tear from her lashes.

"Abby's entitled to get emotional." Maddy went to the stove to pour more coffee. "She's wondering how she's going to feed four extra people for three days. Abby, is there a trick to this stove? I can't get the burner going."

"Push the knob in before you turn it. Can you really stay?" She looked at her mother first because she knew who really called the shots.

"We're between engagements," Molly told her dryly then patted her arm. "If you can put up with us, we'll stay until the end of the week."

"Of course I can put up with you." She hugged Molly again, hardly able to believe her family was in one place at one time. "I only wish Trace were here."

Frank made a hissing sound. "That boy. No sense of responsibility, no ambition. Can't think how I could raise a son to be so feckless."

"It's a mystery." Chantel's dry voice was lost on him.

"He's got talent." Frank slammed his fist on the counter. "Taught him everything I knew. He hasn't walked through a stage door in ten years."

"Did I mention that Chris was in his school Christmas play?" Abby knew how to soothe and distract. "He played a sheep."

Frank positively preened. "A man's got to start somewhere."

"Nice touch, Abby," Maddy murmured.

"Years of practice." She saw Dylan standing slightly off to the side, observing and absorbing—something he did well. She wished she could tell if the smile on his face was one of amusement or disdain. "Coffee?" she asked. He only nodded.

"Dylan, my boy." Frank perked up as he remembered his audience. "Come, sit down here. Let me tell you about the time we played Radio City."

Chantel didn't bother to disguise a moan, and Frank glared at her. "Have some respect."

"Frank, Dylan may not be interested in show business."

Frank looked at his wife as if she'd grown horns. "There's not a person alive who isn't interested in show business." He added two heaping spoonfuls of sugar to his coffee, hesitated briefly, then added a third. "Besides, the man's a writer. That means he likes a story."

"Story's right." Chantel gave her father a loud kiss on the cheek. "Tall story."

Frank raised his chin. "Sit down, Dylan. Ignore the family. I could teach them a time step, but I never could teach them manners."

Frank told his story, interrupted by asides from all three of his daughters and the occasional chuckle from his wife. Dylan would never be sure whether it was fact or fiction, but he was certain that Frank O'Hurley believed every word.

Abby relaxed. Dylan could all but feel the tension that had held her stiff when she'd first come in drain out of her. She seemed to meld with the odd mix of people who were her family. Though she was totally unlike any of them, she fit in like a piece of a jumbled jigsaw puzzle.

He enjoyed them. They were loud, talking over and against each other, laughing at one another. Each one had a habit of grabbing the spotlight and clinging a moment before passing it on. Their stories were exaggerated and dramatic. Yet some of them, though ridiculous, had the ring of truth. Instinctively he found himself making mental notes. The O'Hurleys, singly and as a group, might make a hell of a book.

Not his style, Dylan reminded himself. It wasn't his style at all, of course. But he continued to observe.

When the boys came home, it was chaos. To a casual observer it might have seemed as though the O'Hurleys were competing for the attention of a new audience. Dylan saw something deeper: their innate love of confusion and each other. Ben and Chris were part of

Abby and therefore part of themselves. There were hugs, exclamations, quizzes and presents. Some children might have been overwhelmed by all the sudden attention. Dylan watched as Ben and Chris simply lapped it up as if it were their due. From what he'd gathered, Dylan was certain the boys didn't see their grandparents or their aunts often, but he sensed none of the awkward shyness that might have been expected. At one point, Chris climbed up onto Dylan's lap as though it were his natural place and began bombarding his grandfather with stories of his day at school. Without thinking, Dylan hooked an arm around the boy's waist to secure him. They sat that way for nearly an hour, with the fire crackling in the hearth, the scent of coffee lingering and the echo of voices bouncing off the kitchen walls.

The minute Abby started dinner preparations, Frank was up. Taking both of his grandsons by the hand, he demanded that they take him upstairs and show him some of their more fascinating toys.

Maddy watched them go with a shake of her head. "As quick on his feet as ever."

"The nice thing about your father is that he doesn't consider cooking women's work any more than he considers changing a tire men's work." Molly leaned back in her stool with a smile. "He considers them both work and avoids them at all costs. What can I do, dear?"

"Nothing. This is going to be pretty simple tonight, I'm afraid. Meat loaf."

Chantel walked over and slipped onto a stool in such a way that her skirt flared and settled around her legs. "I guess you want me to peel potatoes or something."

Abby glanced down at her sister's beautifully manicured hands. There was a sunburst of diamonds and sapphires on one finger, and a slim gold watch with an amber face on her wrist. Abby smiled, hefted a bag of potatoes out of the pantry and dropped it on the counter.

"A dozen ought to do it."

With a sigh, Chantel took the paring knife. "I suppose I should learn to keep my mouth shut. You've always been so literal-minded."

Though it would have amused him to watch one of Hollywood's reigning princesses skin potatoes, Dylan rose. "I'll feed the stock."

"But the boys—" Abby began.

"Special circumstances." Dylan grabbed his jacket off the hook.

"I'll give you a hand." Maddy was up and bouncing toward the door. "I'd rather play with the horses than peel potatoes." When the first blast of cool air hit her face, she tossed her head back. "I hope you know your way around the barn. I don't."

"I can manage."

Sigmund bounded around the side of the house and leaped toward her, tongue lolling. Maddy evaded him with the ease of a woman used to dodging foot traffic on crowded sidewalks. She bent down and rubbed his fur vigorously with both hands until he settled down.

"I don't know what to make of you, Dylan." Still leaning over the dog, she turned her head to look up at him. "I'd almost decided not to like you until I saw you with the boys. Generally I think kids are the best judge of people, and they like you." When he said nothing, she straightened and looked directly at him. "The main reason I came down to see Abby was because of you."

Dylan decided the stock could wait, and drew out a cigarette. "I don't think I follow you."

"When I talked to Abby a week or so ago, she sounded unnerved. It takes a lot to unnerve Abby." Maddy dipped her hands into her pockets, but her candid, friendly gaze remained on his. "She's been through a lot. I wasn't always around, Chantel wasn't always around, it wasn't possible to give her support when it turned out she needed it most. That's why we're here now."

He let out a long stream of smoke. "It seems to me that Abby can take care of herself."

"Absolutely." She dragged a hand through her hair, but the wind tossed it back again. "Look at this place. She loves it, and whether she's told you or not, she's done it all on her own. All. I don't know what she's told you, or might tell you, about Chuck Rockwell, but everything here is Abby's."

"You didn't like him."

"For an actress, I'm often transparent. No, I didn't like him, and there are really very few people I can say that about. But my feelings are my own, and Abby's are hers. I won't see her slapped down again, though." She smiled a little, but her smile took nothing away from her firm tone. "Thing is, I'd expected to stand between you and Abby with my fists raised. I don't think that's going to be necessary."

"You don't know me."

"I think Abby does," she said simply. "If she cares for you, there's a reason. I guess that's enough." She linked her arm through his as though she'd been doing so for years. "Let's feed the horses."

Dinner was a babble of conversation. The food might have been simple, but it was consumed enthusiastically, down to the last crumb. When it came time to deal with the dishes, Frank made his escape with his banjo. Because he was entertaining the children, Abby said nothing and went about the task herself. It was reward enough to hear her father's voice over the sound of clattering china and silverware.

"Let me do that."

"Mom, you're on vacation."

"Do you know the last time I washed dishes?" Molly stacked plates in the quick, expert style that demonstrated her on-again, off-again career as a waitress. "God, I don't. I used to think it was relaxing."

Maddy wrinkled her nose and grabbed a few glasses. "I wish you'd come to my apartment and relax. Come on, Chantel, grab that platter."

"I peeled the potatoes," She looked critically at her hands. "Unless you have surgical gloves, I'm not putting these in dishwater."

"Vain," Maddy grumbled as she stacked more dishes. "Always vain."

"It's only vanity if you haven't a right to it." Chantel smiled and slid off the stool. "I think I'll give Pop a hand."

Dylan began to stack plates in the dishwasher. "I imagine you've done enough housework for one day," he said to Abby. "Why don't you go sit with your father?"

One look was enough to remind her of the harsh words he'd spoken that morning. Wanting to avoid a scene in front of her family, Abby backed off. "It looks as though you have things under control."

There was the sound of three-part harmony from the living room. "Frank'll be in heaven," Molly commented. "He's got his girls singing with him again. Go ahead, Maddy, we're nearly done here."

Maddy needed no urging to slip out of the kitchen and into the spotlight. Within seconds the voices were joined by another. Frank picked up the beat with the banjo and went into the next number. Molly began to hum as she wiped off a counter.

"Guess I'm sentimental," she said, "but it does my soul good to hear them."

"You've quite a family, Mrs. O'Hurley."

"Oh, Lord, don't call me that. Call me that and you remind me I'm too damn old to be running around the country and smearing on greasepaint. Molly, just plain Molly."

Dylan closed the door of the dishwasher and looked at her, really looked. She was lovely, with soft, small features and a full, youthful mouth. The lines made no difference that he could see, no difference at all. "I wouldn't say just plain Molly."

She laughed, a full, robust sound that contrasted with her height and build. "Oh, you're a smart one, you are, and you've a way with words. I read your last book, the one about that actress, on the train." She laid the dish-cloth over the spigot.

"And?" There was an *and* in there, though he wasn't certain it would be complimentary.

"You're a hard man, the kind who sees things that would probably be better left alone. But you're fair." When she turned and looked at him again, really looked, he saw that her eyes were like Abby's, deep and vulnerable. "Be fair with my girl, Dylan. That's all I want. She's strong. Sometimes it scares me just how strong. When she's hurt, she doesn't ask for help, but binds her wounds herself. I don't want her to have to bind anymore."

"I didn't come here to hurt her."

"But you may unintentionally hurt her in the end." She sighed a little. Her children were grown. They'd started taking steps without her help years before. "Can you sing?" she asked him abruptly.

Off balance, he looked at her a moment, then laughed. "No."

"Then it's time you learned." She took him by the arm and led him out to join the others.

It was after midnight before the house settled down. Abby thought Maddy and Chantel might still be talking and laughing in the room they were sharing. Her parents would be asleep, as comfortable in the strange bed as they had been in hundreds of other strange beds. She was restless, too restless to sleep, too restless to join her sisters. Instead, she slipped a coat over her robe and went out to the barn. The foal that had pleased Maddy so much was asleep, curled contentedly in the hay with her mother guarding him. Gladys was awake, perhaps too close to her own time to rest. Abby stroked her, hoping to soothe both herself and the mare.

"You need some sleep."

Her fingers tightened in the mare's mane, then slowly relaxed before she turned to Dylan. "I didn't hear you come in. I thought everyone was in bed."

"You should be. You look tired." He came closer, almost afraid to get close enough to touch her. "I saw you leave. I was standing at the window."

"Just checking on Gladys," Abby rested her cheek against the mare's. The morning's argument seemed so far away. It seemed like years since she'd lain beside him and felt excitement build. "With my family here, it's going to be a little difficult for us to work together for the next couple of days."

"I've got enough to work on my own for a while. Abby..." He wanted her, wanted to gather her close and pretend things were every bit as simple as sitting around the living room and singing. He wanted to offer her the kind of unconditional support her family did, yet there seemed to be a wall between them. "I'd like to talk to you about this morning."

She'd known he would. For a moment, she continued to stroke Gladys. "All right. Would you like to go inside?"

"No." He caught her as she turned, caught her before he could give himself the chance to remember he should keep a certain distance. "I want you alone. Damn it, Abby, I want some answers. You're driving me crazy."

"I wish I could give you the ones you want." She took a deep breath and put her hands on his arms, both to comfort, and to emphasize her point. "Dylan, I decided as I was driving back here today to tell you everything, to be completely open with you. I may not give you the answers you want, but I'm going to trust you with the truth."

That was all he wanted from her, or so he told himself. He watched her in the dim, slanting light. "Why?"

She could have evaded him, and perhaps she should have, but honesty had to begin somewhere. "Because I'm in love with you."

He didn't step back, but his hands slid slowly away from her until he was no longer touching her. Abby felt a little tingle of pain. "I told you it might not be the answer you wanted."

"Wait a minute. Wait a minute," he repeated as she turned away. Even through his own shock he'd seen the flicker of hurt in her eyes. "You can't expect to say

something like that and not leave me a little stunned."
When she turned toward him, he didn't reach out to her,
because she terrified him. "I don't know what to say to
you."

"You don't have to say anything." Her words were
calm and low, and there was a touch of amusement in
her eyes now. "I'm responsible for my own feelings,
Dylan. That's something I learned a long time ago. I
answered your question honestly because I decided that
avoiding this and the rest of your questions will only put
me into a hole I may never get out of. About this
morning—"

"The hell with this morning." He caught her face in
his hands and stared at her as though he were seeing her
for the first time. "I don't know what to do about you.
I sure as hell don't know what to do for you."

It would have been so easy just to step forward into
his arms. To ask to be held. She knew he wouldn't re-
fuse. Abby shook her head and kept her arms at her
sides. "That's a problem I can't help you with."

She was closer now, but he didn't even realize that
he'd closed the distance between them. "I don't want to
get tangled up in a relationship. I had one marriage hit
the skids. I have a career that requires me to be selfish
to begin with."

"I'm not asking you for a relationship, Dylan. I'm
not asking you for anything at all."

"That's the trouble, damn it. If you asked, I could
tell you to forget it." Or so he hoped. "If you asked I
could give you two dozen reasons why it would never
work." She looked at him, her eyes warm and calm. He
swore at her, then at himself, before he drew her into his
arms. "I want you. There doesn't seem to be anything
I can do about it."

"There's nothing you have to do."

"Shut up," he muttered. Then he closed his mouth over hers.

It was as if the day had never happened. The heat, the passion, the glow, were just as strong as they'd been before. She softened against him as if she knew he needed her to be soft. Her lips were avid and hungry on his, meeting every demand. In the dim light of the barn he could see her eyes flutter closed, then open to watch him as their mouths met again and again. The scent of animals and hay and leather was strong, but as she entwined her arms around him he could only smell the fresh, light hint of soap on her skin.

"I don't want to talk." He skimmed his lips over her cheek before he drew her back. "I don't really want to think."

"No." She linked her fingers with his. "Not tonight. I'll give you all the answers, Dylan. I promise."

He nodded but wondered if she already had.

Chapter Eleven

Things got a little crazy when Gladys went into labor. Abby was walking through her morning routine, her father strolling along beside her. The ground was hard again and just beginning to show signs of new life. Her father's shoes hit the path in their own cheerful rhythm. She never tired of listening to him spin his stories of life on the road. Even though she'd been there herself for more than half her life, Abby was able to suspend reality and believe it was all glamour and excitement and opening nights.

"I tell you, Abby, it's a great life. City after city, town after town. What a way to see the world."

He never mentioned the back-alley entrances, the smoke-and-liquor-filled rooms, or the disinterested crowds. There were no such things in Frank O'Hurley's world. Abby was grateful for it.

"Vegas, what a place. The neon flashing, the slot machines clinking. People waltzing around in evening clothes at 8:00 a.m. Ah, I'd give a lot to play Vegas again."

"You will, Pop." Maybe not on the Strip, maybe not with his name several feet high on a marquee, but he'd play Vegas again. Just as he'd play in dozens of other towns. A man like Frank O'Hurley couldn't stop performing any more than he could stop breathing and survive. In the blood, he'd often said to her, and in the blood it was. And it was because the O'Hurley blood was thick that he was up before eight o'clock and walking in a farmyard with his daughter when he usually considered noon a barely civilized hour. Knowing that only made Abby love him more.

"This place." He stopped but was careful not to breathe too deeply. "It suits you, I guess. Must take after your grandma. Never would leave that farm in Ireland." He had a moment's pang for early memories that were more dreams than memories. "You happy, Abby?"

She thought about the question because she sensed the answer was important. The farm brought her contentment and personal satisfaction. The children... Abby smiled as she remembered their complaints at being sent off to school when the excitement was at home. The children gave her roots and pride and the kind of love she could never describe. And Dylan. He brought her passion and fire and serenity all at once. He made life complete. Even though she knew it was only temporary, it seemed to be enough.

"I'm happier now that I've been in a long, long time." That was true enough. "I like what I've done here. It's important to me."

It was beyond Frank how anyone could be happy staying rooted to one spot. But he'd always wanted his children to have what they wanted most. It didn't matter what it was, as long as they had it. "This writer..." He felt his way along here. It was untested ground. "Well, Abby, a body would have to be blind not to see the way you look at him."

"I'm in love with him." Strange how easily the words came out now without a pang of regret, without a twinge of fear.

"I see." He let out the whistling sound through his teeth. "Should I talk with him?" For a moment she went blank. Then the laughter came. "Oh, no, Pop, no. You don't have to talk to him." She stopped and kissed her father's smoothly shaven cheek. "I love you."

"And so you should." He pinched her chin. "Now I can admit that your mother and I are concerned about you, living alone out here and trying to run things all on your own." He grinned and tugged on her hair. "Fact is, your mother claims there's not a reason in the world to worry about you, but I worry just the same."

"You don't have to. The boys and I have a good life. The life we want."

"That's easy to say, but a father considers worrying over his daughters a serious matter. Chantel, well, she gave me enough anxiety as a teenager, so I figure we're past that stage now. And Maddy can talk her way in and out of anything under the sun."

"Like her pop."

He grinned. "Like her pop. But you've been a different matter. Never a minute's trouble with you as a child, and then..." He let his words trail off. It wasn't fair or right to tell her now about the hours he'd spend agonizing over what had happened in her life, the heartbreaks, the struggles. Though he was a caring man, he hadn't grieved for his son-in-law. He had only prayed for his daughter's peace of mind. "But now that I know you're going to be settling down with a man, a good, solid man, if I don't miss my mark, I can rest easy.

The early-morning breeze whispered through her hair. It was warm, almost balmy. What a difference a few weeks could make. "I'm not settling down with Dylan, Pop. It's not like that."

"But you just said—"

"I know what I said." She kicked a small stone out of her path and wished other obstacles could be dealt with as easily. "He won't stay, Pop. This isn't the life for him. And I can't go, because this is the life for me."

"I've never heard such a barrel of nonsense." She opened the barn door, and though it hadn't been his intention to actually go in, he was compelled to follow. He'd led his family over the country, crisscrossing, overlapping, circling. Shouldn't he be able to lead his Abby where she already wanted to go? "People in love make certain adjustments. Not sacrifices." Abby knew her father didn't believe in sacrifices. "Compromises and such, Abby. You didn't have that with the other..." He wouldn't say Chuck's name. His throat simply closed over it. "That's because it takes two people to compromise. If one's doing all the adjusting, it's like a rubber band. It's either going to fly away or break."

She studied him. He wasn't a handsome man, but he was an engaging one, with his small, agile build and animated face. Often he played the clown, because bringing laughter was what he felt he'd been fashioned for. But he was no fool.

"You're very wise, Pop." Abby kissed him again and remembered all the times he'd been right there when she'd stumbled. "Dylan's nothing like Chuck. And I'm beginning to realize that I'm nothing like the woman who married that excitingly irresponsible man."

"Just how does this man feel about you?"

"I don't know." She hit the lights. "I guess I really don't want to because it would make the situation harder one way or the other. Now don't worry." She put both hands on his spindly shoulders. "I told you I was happy here just as I am. I'm not looking for a man to take care of me, Pop. I did that once before."

"And a poor job he did of it, too."

She had to laugh and kiss him again. When Frank O'Hurley lost his temper, it was quite a scene. "He wasn't made to take care of me, Pop, and I just couldn't take care of him. You know very well that's not what marriage is about. It's a team, like you and Mom."

"Those two young boys need a man around."

"I know that." That was where the guilt ultimately came from. "I can't give them everything."

He cut himself off because he heard it in her voice, the faint regret, the obvious guilt. He took her hands and squeezed. "You've done a damn fine job with them. Anyone says different, they have to take on Frank O'Hurley."

She laughed, remembering a few brawls. He might be small, but her father enjoyed a tussle. "Why don't you help me feed the horses instead?"

He drew back a little, naturally cautious. "Well, I don't know about that, Abby girl, I'm a man of the city."

"Come on now, you'll want to see the foal."

She started to walk to the first stall when instinct had her looking into Gladys's. With quick moves, Abby was swinging open the stall door and going to the laboring horse.

"What's the matter? What's the matter?" Her father was practically skipping behind her. "Is it sick? Contagious?"

Abby had to laugh even as she checked the mare. "Having babies isn't a communicable disease, Pop. Go into the kitchen, look in my book and call the vet."

He let loose a string of Irish and American curses. "You need water? Hot water?"

"Just call the vet, Pop, and don't worry. I'm an old hand at this."

He scurried off, and didn't come back. Abby hadn't expected him to. He did send Dylan, though to Abby's surprise, Chantel poked her head in the stall behind him.

"Should we get ready to pass out cigars?"

"Soon enough. Did Pop call the vet?"

"I did." Dylan took his place beside her. "Frank ran into the kitchen demanding boiling water. I think your mother's calming him down. How's Gladys doing?"

"Pretty good." She glanced up at her sister. Chantel was as cool and polished as ever in buff-colored slacks and a silk blouse. "You're up early."

Chantel just shrugged, not bothering to mention that when your life revolved around 6:00 a.m. calls you got in the habit of rising early. "I couldn't miss all the excitement." Then, because her heart went out to the mare, female to female, she crouched down. "Anything I can do?"

"It's nearly done," Abby announced.

And so she and Dylan delivered their second foal, working together in a kind of unstated partnership that had Chantel's eyes narrowing. Perhaps she'd misjudged him, she thought. But she wasn't accustomed to misjudging a man. Not any longer.

"What's going on?"

Rumpled from a night's sleep and dressed in overalls that swamped her, Maddy staggered in. "I'm supposed to bring a message to the front. It seems the vet's on call. His service is tracking him down, but it might be a while." She yawned hugely. "Pop's got water boiling on every burner. If the vet doesn't show up soon he's threatening to call the paramedics. You can't even get a cup of coffee in there."

"We're getting ready to knit four little pink bootees," Chantel told her. She brushed off the knees of her slacks as she rose.

"Would you look at that." Maddy focused her sleep-bleared eyes on the foal. "Hey, wait, don't anybody move. I've got to go get my camera. The guys in dance class won't believe it." She was off and running.

"Well, now that the excitement's over I think I'll just toddle inside and see if I can get Pop to give up some of his boiling water. I'm dying for coffee." Chantel sauntered off, trailing a tantalizing scent behind her.

"Your family's something," Dylan murmured.

"Yeah." Abby wiped sweat from her face with her shirtsleeve. "I know."

When Maddy suggested riding, Abby rearranged her schedule and saddled Judd. Dylan was working and her parents weren't interested, so it would be the three of them, as it so often had been in the past. She watched

Maddy adjust a stirrup with breezy confidence before she turned to Chantel.

"Need some help?"

"Oh, I think I can manage." Chantel fastened the cinch on the little mare.

"I didn't think you rode at all." Cautious, Abby rechecked the saddle. "But Matilda here is gentle."

Chantel adjusted the collar of her blouse. "We'll just poke along."

Once outside, Maddy swung into the saddle with athletic ease. Chantel hesitated, fumbled and finally managed to mount the mare. Abby decided to keep Judd to a walk beside her sister. "We can go up this road. It runs along the east side of the property where we'll be planting hay in a couple of weeks."

"Planting hay." Chantel's mare stood soberly while she looked lazily around. "How rural of you."

Maddy chuckled. "Okay, Miss Hollywood, let's ride."

Chantel shifted down in the saddle. "Better, Miss New York, let's race." As Abby's mouth dropped open, Chantel pressed her heels to the mare's sides and lunged forward. Maddy started to shout a warning, then realized it wasn't necessary. Chantel was laughing and riding beautifully.

"Always full of surprises," Maddy said to Abby.

Abby skimmed her own heels over Judd. "What are we waiting for?"

For more than half a mile she rode free, easily matching Maddy's pace. It brought memories of childhood. Chantel had always been the leader then, as well. Even with the grueling schedules of trains and buses and one-night stands, they'd managed to fight and play like most children. Even prior to birth, they'd had each other. Nothing had changed that.

They pulled up, breathless and laughing, where Chantel waited at the top of the crest.

"Where'd you learn to ride like that?" Maddy demanded.

Chantel simply fluffed her hair. "Darling, just because you gulp vitamins and jog ten miles a day doesn't mean you're the only O'Hurley with any athletic ability." When Maddy snorted, she grinned. The Hollywood actress was gone, and Chantel was just a woman enjoying a joke. "I've just come off a Western, Wyoming circa 1870." She arched her back and rolled her eyes. "I swear I spent more time in the saddle than any cattle rustler. Lost a half inch off my hips."

Abby controlled Judd as he danced sideways. "It's not all flashy premieres and lunches at Ma Maison, is it?"

"No." Then she tossed her hair back and shrugged. "But you do what you do best, it you're smart. Isn't that what you're doing?"

Abby glanced around the land she'd fought so hard to keep. "Raising children and planting hay. Yes, I suppose it's what I do best."

"I can't say I envy you, but I do admire you." They began to walk the horses, Chantel in the middle, Abby to the left and Maddy to the right, in the same position they'd used before more audiences than they could have counted.

Maddy adjusted the stride of her horse to match her sisters'. "Do you remember that time in that little place just outside Memphis?"

"The place where all the customers drank straight bourbon and looked as though they could chew raw meat?'' Abby shook her hair back and looked at the sky. ''God, it's hard to believe we lived through that one.''

''Lived through it,'' Chantel repeated, buffing her nails on her suede jacket. ''Darling, we were a smash.''

''Yeah, there were about six bottles smashed that night, as I recall.''

Remembering made Maddy chuckle. ''On opening night I pretend I'm about to play in Mitzie's Place outside Memphis. I tell myself whatever happens can't be as bad.''

''What are you going to do when you get back?'' Abby asked her. ''Are you really leaving *Suzanna's Park*? It looks like it'll have a long run on Broadway.''

''Over a year of dancing the same routines, saying the same words.'' Maddy clicked to her horse as he took an interest in the shrubbery on the side of the road. ''I wanted something new, and as it turned out, there's a play in the works now. If they find an angel, we could be in rehearsals in a couple months. I'm a stripper.''

''A what?'' Chantel and Abby said in unison.

''A stripper. You know, bump, grind, take it off. The character's wonderful, a lady of free spirit and morals who meets the guy of her dreams and pretends she's a librarian. And no, I won't actually bare my full talent on stage. We want to bring in the family crowd, as well.''

''What about you, Chantel? Taking a break?'' Abby asked.

''Who could stand it? I'm going to start shooting a miniseries in about ten days. Did you read *Strangers*?''

''God, yes, it was wonderful. I thought...'' Maddy's words trailed off, and her eyes widened. ''You're going to play Hailey. Oh, Chantel, what a wonderful part. Abby, did you read it?''

"No, I don't get a lot of time to read anymore." It was said simply, without malice.''

"It's all about this—"

"Maddy." Chantel cut her off as they rode beside a big spreading elm. "Let's not give her the whole story line. You can watch it in the comfort of your own home in a few months, Abby."

It no longer surprised her that she could indeed snuggle on the living room sofa and watch her sister on television. "Somehow I never thought you'd do TV again," Abby commented.

"Neither did I, but the script was too good. Anyway, it might be interesting to go back." She rarely admitted she liked challenges. The image of glamour and ease had been too hard-won. "I haven't worked the small screen since my sensuous-shampoo and brighter-than-white-toothpaste ads." They were far enough away from the house now, and Abby seemed relaxed. Chantel and Maddy exchanged a glance. Agreement needed no words.

"What about you, Abby?" Chantel tugged on the reins and skirted around easily to put Abby in the middle. "What's the story with you and Crosby?"

"The story," she said simply, "*is* what Dylan came here to write. I have to tell it, at least parts of it."

"Does feeling the way you do about him make it easier?"

Abby absorbed Maddy's question. She didn't have to tell either of her sisters that she was in love. They could feel it almost as strongly as she did. "In some ways. I'd planned to, well...I guess I'd planned to restructure the facts. That doesn't work with Dylan, because he knows just by looking at me whether or not I'm being up-front with him. So I have to tell him the truth.''

Chantel felt her temper start to rise. ''Have you told him what a bitch Janice Rockwell is? How she treated you and the boys after Chuck died?''

''That's not really relevant, is it?''

''Well, I for one would like to read it in black and white,'' Maddy muttered. ''What she did was criminal.''

''What she did was perfectly within the law,'' Abby corrected. ''Just because it wasn't right doesn't mean it wasn't legal. Anyway, I think I'm better off the way things turned out. Made me shape up.''

''I think he should know it all,'' Chantel insisted. ''All the details, all the angles. Race driver's wealthy mother leaves widow and children impoverished.''

''Oh, Chantel, it wasn't as bad as that. We were hardly begging for pennies.''

''It was as bad as that,'' she corrected. ''Abby, if you're going to trust him with some, you should trust him with everything.''

''She's right.'' Maddy was silent a moment. The sun was warm and bright, the scent of new grass pungent, but she could sense the turmoil within her sister. ''I thought the whole idea was a mistake, but now that it's being done, it should be done properly. Look, I know there were plenty of things you didn't tell us. You didn't have to. Don't you think you'd feel better, feel freer, if you finally got it all out?''

''I'm not thinking of me. I've learned to deal with it. I'm thinking of the boys.''

''Do you think they don't know?'' Chantel said quietly.

"No." She looked down at her hands, voicing what she'd been avoiding for the longest time. "They know; not the details, but they've sensed the mood. What they don't know now they'll find out sooner or later. I just want Dylan to write it with enough compassion so when they're old enough they can accept it all."

"Does he have any?" Chantel asked her.

"Any what?"

"Compassion."

"Yes." Abby smiled then, relaxing again. "A surprisingly large amount."

That was something Chantel intended to test for herself. "How does he feel about you?"

"He cares." In unspoken agreement, they turned the horses back. "I think he cares more than he ever bargained for, not only about me but the kids. It won't make any difference when he's finished. He'll leave."

"Then you have to make him stay."

Abby smiled at Maddy. "You got all the optimism. Chantel got all the guile."

"Thank you very much." Only half-amused, Chantel picked up the pace.

"Maddy can just believe strongly enough and things happen. You make them happen. I just shuffle around the cards I've been dealt until I have the best hand I can manage. I can't make Dylan stay, because if he asked, I couldn't go. I'm not eighteen and impulsive anymore. I have two children."

Chantel held her head high and let the wind take her hair. It was a sensation of absolute freedom she couldn't often allow herself. "I don't see why you should make him stay in the first place. Some women put too much emphasis on having a man complete their lives. They should be fulfilled in the first place—then a man might be a nice addition."

"Spoken like a true heartbreaker," Maddy put in.

"I don't break hearts." Chantel smiled slowly. "I only bruise them a little."

"I'll gag any minute," Maddy said to her horse. "In any case, just because you and I aren't ready to settle down doesn't mean that Abby isn't entitled to dirty dishes in the sink and someone to take out the garbage."

"An interesting description of a meaningful relationship," Abby murmured. "As the only one of the three of us who's ever been married, I feel qualified to say that there's a bit more to it than that."

"Hold on, Abby." Concerned, Chantel slowed her horse. "Who's talking marriage? I'm not saying you shouldn't have a good time with him, enjoy him, certainly, but you can't seriously be thinking about locking yourself in again."

"Another interesting description," Maddy commented, making Abby laugh.

"If I thought we had a shot at it and if I could find a foothold for compromise, I'd ask him myself."

"Then go for it." The sun shot a halo around Maddy's bright, rumpled hair. "If you love him, if he's right for you, why anticipate problems?"

Chantel gave a quick, amused laugh. "The bulk of this woman's experience with men has been limited to socializing with dancers who stand in front of mirrors all day and admire themselves."

"Dylan's not a dancer," Maddy pointed out, unbruised. "And the actors you spend time with can't figure out who they really are after a day on the set."

"Jaded." Abby shook her head and struggled not to laugh. "I think all of us better stay single."

"Amen to that," Chantel breathed.

"Who has time for romance, anyway?" Maddy commented. "Between dance classes, rehearsals and matinees, I'm too tired for candlelight and roses. Who needs men?"

"Darling, that depends on whether you're talking about a permanent addition or an occasional escort."

"You're starting to believe your own press," Abby said as the house came into view.

"Why shouldn't I?" Chantel lifted a brow. "Everyone else does." With a laugh and a kick of her heels, she plunged ahead.

"Damned if she's going to beat me again!" Maddy was off like a shot.

Abby took a moment to smile after them before she signaled to Judd, knowing his long, powerful stride would bring her in ahead of her sisters.

Chapter Twelve

The moonlight was soothing, thin white, and quiet as it fell over the bed. The house, though silent, almost seemed to ring with the echo of voices and laughter, music—the music her family created wherever they went. Her mother playing the banjo while her father danced. Her father playing while all of them sang. Tomorrow they would be gone, but Abby thought it would be a long time before those echoes faded completely.

Content but far from sleepy, she cradled her head on Dylan's shoulder and just listened.

It was silly, she supposed, to feel as though she was stealing this time with him. With her family in the house, being with him was like walking on eggshells. He must have felt something of it as well. Now he came to her late at night, after the others were asleep, and left early, at first light.

They hadn't discussed it. He'd seemed to have understood that she would feel awkward. She was a grown woman, a widow, the mother of two, but she felt entirely too much like a daughter when her parents were under the same roof.

They might laugh about it later, but for now the echoing silence was too lovely.

He was listening to his own echoes. The phone calls he'd made while Abby had been occupied with her family had added more pieces to the puzzle. He didn't like all of them. When her family was gone the questions would start again, but he already had a number of answers.

It was more important to him now that she tell him things he was already aware of, that she trusted him with secrets he already knew. When she did, if she did, maybe they could put yesterdays behind them and deal with tomorrows.

"Are you asleep?"

"No." He brushed his lips over her hair. Tonight was the last night for pretenses, and he wanted badly to give her whatever she needed. "I was thinking of your parents. I've never met anyone like them."

"I'm not sure there is anyone like them." It pleased her. Abby let her eyes half close as memories fluttered through her head.

"The only thing that scared me was that your father was really insisting he could teach me to tap-dance."

"The thing is, Pop could teach anyone to dance. I'm living proof." She yawned and settled more comfortably against him.

"They'll take the limo to the bus station and travel to Chicago."

"For a three-day gig." She smiled a little, picturing them going over their routine in a cramped motel room. "Chantel wanted to put them on a plane, first class. They wouldn't hear of it. Mom said she'd managed to get where she was going for fifty years without leaving the ground and saw no reason to start now."

"Your mother's a sensible woman."

"I know. Sort of a contradiction in terms, isn't it? I think if she ever found herself in suburbia, with a lawn and a chain-link fence, she'd go crazy. She found the perfect partner when she hooked up with Pop."

"How long have they been together?"

"Hmmm. About thirty-five years now."

He was silent for a moment. "Kind of lifts your confidence in the institution."

"I think one of the reasons I married so quickly was that Mom and Pop made it seem so easy. For them, it really is. I'm going to miss them."

He heard the wistfulness in her voice and drew her closer. "Never a dull moment. I thought you were going to lose a couple of lamps when Frank decided to teach the boys how to juggle."

Abby turned her face into his shoulder as she laughed. "There won't be an apple worth eating until Ben gets it out of his system."

"Better than having him throw them at Chris."

"Every time." She lifted her head, and though she was still smiling, her eyes were serious as she looked down at him. "I'm glad you were here to meet them. Someday you might be traveling through some small, half-forgotten town and see their names on a marquee. You'll remember me."

In a habit he knew would be hard to break, he combed his fingers through her hair. "Do you think I'll need a marquee?"

"It wouldn't hurt." Lowering her mouth, she let it linger on his, warm and sweet. "I'd like to think you'd remember this." She brushed her hand through his hair, then skimmed her lips over his temple. "And that."

"I've a good memory, Abby." He took her wrists. The pulses in them were just beginning to quicken. "A very good memory."

Still holding her, he rolled over, pinning her body with his. There it was, instantly, that splinter of excitement, that calming feeling of rightness. With his lips, he found hers. He didn't release her hands. Not yet. Somehow he knew if she touched him then, he'd explode, go mad, take frantically what he wanted to savor. They had all night, they had years. If he believed hard enough, they had forever. So he held himself a prisoner as much as he held her, letting his lips soothe, arouse and entice.

He sucked at her tongue, drawing it deep into his mouth, teasing it with his own. Feeling her breath shudder against his mouth, he groaned at the sensation. At each move, her body sank into the mattress, strong enough to take, pliant enough to give. Still holding her wrists, he skimmed down the long line of her throat. There was pulse hammering, a flavor tempting. He could have spent hours exploring each tiny spot where her blood pulsed close to the surface. He felt at home. Her body offered him both peace and rest, passion and excitement. He had only to take what he needed most.

She loved him. It was a wild, terrifying thought. Yet when he released her wrists her arms wrapped around his so naturally, hands soothing and tormenting all at once. She asked for nothing, and by doing so asked for more than he'd thought he could ever give again.

He was so gentle. Abby wondered if she'd ever get used to the quiet tenderness beneath the fire. His hands molded, caressed. At times his fingers dug unheedingly into her flesh, but there was always such underlying care, such overlying sweetness.

Whenever she heard his breath grow uneven, she was amazed. She reveled in feeling his muscles quiver and tense beneath her exploring hands. It was for her, from her, with her. Never before, not even in her dreams, had there been a man with such a compelling need for her.

Yet she wondered if he knew. Even as they took each other deep and fast, feeling the blood heat the surface of their skin, she wondered if he knew what that beyond wanting her, beyond desiring her, he needed her in his life.

Unless he did, their relationship would end when he had his answers. And she'd already promised to give them to him.

"Dylan." The sudden stark realization ran through her that he was slipping through her fingers just when she'd learned to grab hold. She had no tricks, no wiles, knew no secret ways to keep a man and bind him to her. She could only give him what was in her heart and hope it was enough for both of them.

He heard his name come softly from her. He felt the sigh run deep inside her. Because he felt she needed it, he brought his lips back to hers and let her take what she wanted.

"Slowly." He slipped inside her, cushioning her gasp with his mouth. "I want to watch you climb, Abby."

The flickers of passion, of pleasure, of wonder on her face aroused him more than he'd ever imagined possible. He'd thought he wasn't the sort of man to give, but with her he was driven to. For years he'd taken, sometimes carelessly, often selfishly. It was never like that with Abby. It left him shaken. It left him wondering.

Between packing, last-minute details and Saturday-morning cartoons, everyone in the house was occupied. Chantel bided her time. When Dylan went to help the boys tend the stock, she waited a few moments, then slipped out to join them. It was warm for March by East Coast standards, but she shivered inside her jacket and decided she'd be glad to get back to Southern California. Before she went, she had something to do.

Most of the horses were in the paddock. Chantel wandered over to lean on the fence. He'd come out sooner or later. She could wait.

Dylan let out the two geldings and saw her. He'd known for days that she had something to say to him. It appeared the time was now. He released the horses and carefully closed the gate behind them. In silence he moved over and joined her at the fence. She took the cigarette he offered. She rarely smoked; it all had to do with mood. She inhaled deeply then let out a long stream of smoke, watching the horses as she spoke.

"I haven't decided if I like you. It's not really important. Abby's feelings are."

Dylan decided she couldn't know how closely her words echoed Maddy's. It was just part of the bond. Together they watched as Eve's foal began to nurse. The mare steadied herself against the pull and tug, then stood patiently.

"I can tell you I didn't like you when you interviewed me about Millicent Driscoll for your last book. Some of it had to do with that period of my life, and the rest was your attitude. I found you abrasive and unsympathetic, so I wasn't as open with you as I might have been. If I had been, maybe you'd have found a little more room for compassion in your story. But Abby's my sister."

For the first time, she turned to look at him. Even in the strong, unrelenting sunlight, her face was stunning. The classic oval shape, the sweep of cheekbone, the flawless skin. A man could look at that face and forget there was anything else to the woman. But it was her eyes that held his interest. He imagined they'd ruthlessly flayed a great many men.

"I think you care about Abby, but I'm not sure if you're too tough to let that matter. I want to tell you about Chuck Rockwell in a way I don't think Abby can." She drew in more smoke, appreciating its rough taste. "This is off-the-record, Dylan. If Abby consents to this you can use anything I say. If she doesn't, you're out of luck. Agreed?"

"Agreed. Tell me."

"When Chuck came into the club that first night, he was utterly infatuated with Abby. Maybe, for a little while, he was even in love with her. I don't know the kind of women he'd been running with before, but I can imagine. Abby, was, even with the tacky costume and greasepaint, untouched. Gullible's a hard word unless you understand the person, and Abby was and still is gullible." She smiled, not the clever, ice-edged smile she used so often but a simple, easy curving of the lips that was as beautiful as it was revealing. "She believed in love, devotion, till death us do part. She went into marriage with stars in her eyes.''

He could imagine Abby then, open, innocent, trusting. "And Rockwell?''

"He loved her, I think, as far as he was capable and for as long as he was capable. Some people say weakness doesn't make a person bad.'' Something flickered in her eyes but was quickly masked. "I disagree with that. Chuck was weak emotionally. I could make excuses for him, knowing that he was raised by an impossibly domineering mother and a workaholic father. Personally, I don't care much for excuses.''

She glanced over, waiting for him to comment. "Go on.'' Dylan had already researched Rockwell's upbringing.

"They had trouble almost from the start. She'd cover it up, but it's difficult to hide anything from another triplet. She went with him to Paris, London, wore beautiful clothes and was offered the sort of life-style a lot of women dream of. Not Abby.'' Chantel shook her head, and her fingers began to drum lightly on the fence rail. "I'm not saying she didn't enjoy it at first, but Abby had always looked for roots. The O'Hurleys have a difficult time sinking them.''

"That's why she wanted this place.''

Chantel dropped her cigarette on the ground and left it to smolder. "Chuck bought it after a particularly messy affair with a girl too young to know any better. Then, almost as soon as he did, he grew bored with it. He made it clear to Abby that if she wanted to keep the place and maintain it she had to do it herself.''

"She told you that?''

"No. Chuck did.'' She sent him an odd, self-mocking look. "He breezed into L.A. and decided it might be interesting to put the moves on his wife's sister. Charming. Give me another cigarette."

While he lit if for her, Chantel composed herself. "As it happened, he wasn't my type, and though my morals are often in doubt, I do have standards. He did manage to get drunk and tell me all the problems he was having with the little woman at home. She was boring." Chantel blew out a vicious stream of smoke. "She was too ordinary, too middle-class. She'd dug into this farm and was holding on, and he had better things to do with his money. If she wanted the damn roof fixed, she could deal with it herself. If she wanted the plumbing brought up to twentieth-century standards, she'd just have to figure out how to manage it on her own. He wasn't interested. He went on about how she had this wild idea to raise horses. He laughed at her." Chantel's jaw stiffened. When she realized she was speaking too quickly, she deliberately slowed. "I didn't throw him out, because I wanted to hear it all. While she'd been going through this, I'd been busy carving out my own career. Too busy, you see, to pay much attention, even though I knew instinctively that things weren't right with Abby."

And how much attention had *he* really paid over the past weeks? That thought stung him. He'd expected her trust and honesty—had demanded it—but all he'd given her were questions.

He'd seen her, listened to her, watched her, and he'd known in his gut that all the preconceptions he'd come with were wrong. Yet why had she stayed with Rockwell? And why did he hate himself for still needing to know?

He drew back, "Why do you think he told you all this?" he asked his voice unemotional.

Her look was hard. It was amazing how quickly her expression could change from cool to frigid without her moving a muscle. "Obviously he thought I'd be just as amused as he." She smiled again and drew more calmly on her cigarette. "Anyway, I got rid of him, then I called Maddy and we came here. Abby was living in a place that was nearly ready to fall down around her ears. Chuck wasn't giving her a dime, so she was working part-time at places she could take Ben along. She was glad to see us, but she wasn't ready to listen to any advice that led to divorce."

"Why?" Dylan touched her for the first time, just a hand on her arm, but she could feel the intensity of his response. "Why did she stay with him?"

So, that was the crux of it, Chantel realized. He cared, and that made it difficult to hold her grudge against him. "I think you'll need to get that answer from her, but I can tell you this. Abby has a large capacity for hope, and she kept believing that Chuck would come around. Meantime, there was the immediate problem of making the house livable. We went to Richmond and sold her jewelry. Chuck had been very generous in the first six or eight months of their marriage and it brought in enough to get her going. I bought her mink." What she didn't mention was that she hadn't been able to afford it at the time. "She joked later that she saw a picture of me wearing her roof."

"She sold the mink to fix the roof," he murmured.

"There were a lot of repairs. It amazed me then how stubborn she was about this place. But when I see her here now, it's obvious how right it is for her and the kids. After that, things settled down a bit. She was pregnant with Chris. I have my own theory on that, but it's best left alone."

He looked at her and saw that she understood more than Abby would ever have guessed. "It's being left alone."

"Maybe I do like you." She relaxed a little and tossed the cigarette aside. "After Chris was born, things went from bad to worse. Chuck was blatant about his affairs. I don't consider it a point in his credit, but I believe he wanted to push Abby into a divorce for her own good. When she did, when she finally did, I think he realized just how much he was losing."

"Are you saying that Abby had filed for divorce?"

"That's right. She could have raked him over the coals—I certainly would have—but she didn't charge him with adultery and she didn't ask for alimony. All she wanted was the farm and some reasonable support for the kids. He was involved with Lori Brewer at the time, and they went on quite a binge. Somewhere along the line, it must have hit him. He'd compensated for the loss of the thrill of racing with other things. He'd had a wife who'd stuck by him and two wonderful children he'd traded for a life-style that only led to more misery. I know how he felt because he called me a few days before that last race. God knows why. I was hardly sympathetic. He said he'd called Abby and had asked her to reconsider and she'd refused. He wanted me to go to bat for him. I told him to grow up. A couple days later, he crashed."

"And she was left feeling guilty because she'd planned to divorce him."

"You catch on." She tapped a beautifully manicured nail against the rail. "There's never been any use telling her not to feel that way, or not to let herself be punished."

Dylan was having problems enough with his own sense of guilt, but he focused on Chantel's last words. "What do you mean, punished?"

"Did you ever consider how difficult it is to maintain a place like this, to raise two children—I'm not speaking of emotionally or physically now, but financially."

"Rockwell had plenty of money."

"Rockwell did—Janice Rockwell did, and she still does. Abby didn't get a penny." She shook her head before he could interrupt her. Every time she thought of it she tasted venom. "She saw to it that Abby didn't get a penny of Chuck's trust fund, not for herself, not for the farm, not for the children."

While Chantel tasted venom, something like acid rose in Dylan's throat. Everything he'd said to Abby from the first day in the rain dreary kitchen to the morning he'd watched her drop rubber gloves in her purse came back to him. And he realized, as his stomach twisted, that he'd have to live with that.

"How has she managed to hold on to the farm?"

"She took out a loan."

There was a bitter taste in his mouth that had nothing to do with tobacco. He hadn't believed in her, hadn't trusted his own feelings enough. She'd been too proud to tell him the things Chantel was saying now.

The hell with her pride, he thought suddenly, viciously. Didn't he have a right to know? Didn't he have a right to... Checking his thoughts, he stared over the paddock and to the hills beyond. No, it was *his* pride that was bruised, he realized, both the man's and the reporter's. She'd known what he'd thought of her, and she'd accepted it—and him.

"Why are you telling me this?"

"Because someone has to convince Abby that it wasn't her fault, that she couldn't have prevented anything that happened. I think you're the one to do it. I think you're the man, if you've got the spine for it, to make her happy."

Her chin was up, her eyes dark as she tossed the challenge at him. Dylan found himself smiling. "You're a hell of a woman. I missed that the first time around."

She smiled back. "Yeah. I missed a few things about you, too."

Maddy stuck her head out of the back door. "Chantel, the limo's here."

"I'm coming." She took a step back, then gave him one last piercing look. "One more thing, Dylan. If you hurt Abby, you're going to have to deal with me."

"Fair enough."

He offered his hand. As though she were amused by both of them, Chantel accepted it. "I guess I'll wish you luck."

"I appreciate it."

The goodbyes were long, tearful and noisy. Maddy came to Dylan and gave him a surprisingly hard and affectionate hug. "Lucky for you I think you're good for her," she whispered in his ear. Then she backed off with a smile. "Welcome to the family, Dylan."

Each member made the rounds twice before climbing into the limo. Chris and Ben had to be coaxed out once they discovered all the knobs and automatic buttons inside the car. After they'd raised and lowered the windows half a dozen times, blasting the stereo and the sleek compact TV, Abby pulled them out so that the rest of her family could climb in. Serene as an ocean liner, the limo cruised up the rut-filled lane.

"I'm going to drive a limo," Chris decided on the spot. "I can wear a neat hat like the one Mr. Donald had and ride in the front seat."

"I'd rather ride in the back with the TV."

Laughing, Abby ruffled Ben's hair. "There's a lot of O'Hurley in this boy. I don't know about you, but I want something long and cold before I tackle the mess in the kitchen."

"Can we go play with the foals?" Ben was already off the porch as he asked.

"Not too rough," Abby called after them. With a sigh, she turned into the house. "I miss them already."

"Quite a family."

"To say the least. Do you want a soda?"

"No." Restless, he wandered around the kitchen. Chantel's words were still eating at him. That, and everything else he'd learned over the last couple of days. The fact that he'd misjudged Abby so completely and so unfairly left him unsure of himself. "Abby, this place, the farm, it's very important to you."

"Aside from the boys, it's the most important." She filled a glass with ice.

"You're not a pushover." He said it so strongly that she turned back to stare at him.

"I don't like to think so."

"Why did you let Rockwell push you around?" he demanded. "Why did you let his mother push you out of everything you were entitled to?"

"Wait a minute." She'd expected a day, even a few hours, before she had to plunge into it all again. "Janice had virtually nothing to do with the rest of it, certainly nothing to do with Chuck's biography."

"The hell with the biography." He took her by the arms. It wasn't until that moment that he realized the book meant nothing, had meant nothing for some time. Abby meant everything. He could only see what she'd been through, what she had done, what had been done to her. If she wouldn't hate, he would hate for her. "She made certain you didn't get a penny of Rockwell's trust fund. With that money the farm would have been free and clear. You were entitled, your children were entitled. Why did you tolerate that?"

"I don't know where you got your information." She struggled to keep her voice calm. There had been bitterness long ago, and she'd swallowed it. She had no desire to taste it again. "Janice had control of the trust. Chuck would have inherited at thirty-five, but he didn't live that long. The money was hers."

"Do you really think that would have stood up in court?"

"I wasn't interested in going to court. Chuck left us some money."

"What was left after he'd blown most of it away."

Abby nodded, keeping her voice even. This was an old argument, one she'd had with herself years before. "Enough so I can be sure that the kids can go to college."

"In the meantime you had to take out a loan just to keep a roof over their heads."

It humiliated her. He couldn't know how it had humiliated her to ask for money, how it embarrassed her that Dylan was now aware of it. "Dylan, that isn't your concern."

"I'm making it my concern. You're my concern. Do you know how it made me feel to know that you're scrubbing some woman's floors?"

She let out an impatient huff of air. "What difference does it make whose floors I scrub?"

"It makes a big difference to me because I don't want you—I can't stand thinking of you..." He swore and tried again. "You could have been honest with me, maybe not at first, but later, after we'd come to mean something to each other."

To mean *what*? she wanted to ask. At least she'd been honest about her feelings. She took the coffeepot from the stove and calmly moved to the sink to fill it with soapy water. "I was as honest as I could be. If it had only been me, I might have told you everything, but I had to think of the boys."

"I wouldn't do anything to hurt them. I couldn't."

"Dylan, why should any of this be important?" She wasn't calm, she thought. Damn it, she wasn't calm at all. She could feel anger building up and throbbing in her head. "It's only money. Can't you just let it go?"

"It's not just about money, and no, I can't let it go. You haven't let it go either or you'd have been able to tell me about it." The frustration hit him, the guilt, the anger. And suddenly he flashed back to the picture of her, wrapped like a princess in white fur. "You sold that damn white mink to fix the roof."

Baffled, she shook her head. "What difference does that make? I hardly need a mink to feed the stock."

"You knew what I thought of you." Dylan's anger with himself only made him more unreasonable with her. "You let me go on thinking that. Even when I was busy falling in love with you, you never really trusted me with all of it. Double-talk and evasions, Abby. You never told me you were going to divorce him, you never told me you had to struggle just to keep food on the table. Do you know how it makes me feel to find out all of these things in bits and pieces?"

"Do you know how it makes me feel?" Her voice rose to match his. "Do you know how it feels to rake it all up, to remember what a miserable failure I was?"

"That's ridiculous. You have to know how foolish that statement is."

"I know how foolish I was."

"Abby." His tone roughened, but his hands grew gentle on her arms. "*He* failed you, he failed his children, and he failed himself." He gave her a quick shake, desperate to make her see what she'd done and how much he respected her for it. "You were the one who made things work. You're the one who built a home and a life."

"Stop yelling at my mom."

Rigid and pale, Ben stood just inside the kitchen doorway. Already upset, Abby could do little more than stare at him. "Ben—"

"Let go of my mom." His bottom lip quivered, but the look he sent Dylan was devastatingly man-to-man. "Let go of her and go away. We don't want you here."

Disgusted with himself, Dylan released Abby and turned to the boy. "I wouldn't hurt your mother, Ben."

"You were, I saw you."

"Ben." Abby stepped between them quickly. "You don't understand. We were angry with each other. People sometimes yell at each other when they're angry."

His jaw was set in a way that reminded Abby almost painfully of her father in full temper. "I don't want him to yell at you. I'm not going to let him hurt you."

"Honey, I was yelling back." She said it softly, dropping her hand to stroke his head. "And he wasn't hurting me."

His eyes shone with a mixture of humiliation and anger. "Maybe you like him better than me."

"No, baby—"

"I'm not a baby!" His pale face filled with color as he pushed away. "I'll show you!" Abby was still crouched on the floor as the back door slammed behind him.

"Oh, God." Slowly Abby rose to her feet. "I didn't handle that very well."

"It was my fault." Dylan dragged both hands through his hair. He'd wanted to give, to offer whatever he could to all of them. Instead, he'd managed to hurt Abby and alienate Ben in one instant. "Let me go talk to him."

"I don't know. Maybe I should—oh, my God! Ben, Ben, stop!" She was through the back door before Dylan could call out. He was behind her in an instant, then past her. Ben was mounted on top of Thunder, and the high-strung stallion was bucking nastily.

Abby's heart lodged in her throat as the boy clung to the horse's back and she couldn't even call his name again. For a moment she thought he'd be able to control the horse and slip off safely, but then the stallion reared so violently that for an instant horse and boy were one form, raised high against the blue sky behind them. Then Ben was tossed off as carelessly as a fly.

She heard his cry mingle with the shrill whinnies of the animal. Slowly, as if suspended in time, she watched, devastated, as hooves danced around Ben's body, miraculously missing him. She tasted her own fear, which rose like rust in her mouth as she raced over the last few feet of ground.

"Ben. Oh, Ben." She wasn't weeping, but along with Dylan began to check his limp body for signs of life.

"He's okay, but he's unconscious. I think his arm's broken." His own hands were shaking. If he'd only been quicker, just a few seconds... "Abby, can you pull the car around?"

Ben lay quietly, his face pale as milk. She wanted to cover his body with hers and weep. "Yes." Glancing up, she saw Chris standing beside her, shaking like a leaf. "Come on, Chris." She took his hand in hers. "We've got to take Ben to the hospital."

"Is he okay? Is he going to be okay?"

"He's going to be fine," she murmured as she hurried for the car.

"Can you drive?" Dylan asked her when she came back. "I don't know the way."

With a nod, she helped him settle her firstborn on his lap in the front seat. Teeth set, she went slowly down the lane, terrified of jolting him with bumps. The moment she got onto the highway, she pressed the accelerator and stopped thinking.

When Ben stirred, she felt tears well up and forced them back. The first whimpering sounds he made became full-fledged sobbing as he regained consciousness fully. She began to talk to him, nonsense, anything that came into her head. From the back seat, Chris leaned up and tentatively stroked Ben's leg. Not knowing what else to do, Dylan held the boy tight in his arms and brushed gently at his hair.

"Almost there, Ben," he murmured. "Just hang on."

"It hurts."

"Yeah, I know." When the boy turned his face into his shirt, Dylan held on. For the first time in his life, he fully understood what it meant to feel someone else's pain.

Abby left the car by the curb outside the emergency room and leaped out to help Dylan with Ben.

It seemed to take hours. Her teeth began to chatter as she gave the admissions clerk insurance information and Ben's medical history. She took deep, gulping breaths and tried to compose herself when they wheeled Ben away for X rays. Her little boy had tried, in his angry way, to prove he was a man. Now he was hurt, and she could only wait. Beside her, Dylan stood holding Chris in his arms.

"Sit down, Abby. It's bound to take some time."

"He's just a little boy." She couldn't fall apart now. Ben was going to need her. But the tears poured out and ran silently down her cheeks. "He was so angry. He'd never have gotten on the stallion if he hadn't been angry."

"Abby, boys are always breaking bones." But his own stomach was knotted and rolling.

"What's going to happen to Ben?" When he saw his mother's tears, Chris's breath began to hitch.

"He's going to be all right." Abby pushed both hands over her cheeks to dry them. "The doctors are taking care of him."

"I think he's going to have a cast." Dylan ran his hands down Chris's short, sturdy arm. "When it's dry you can sign your name on it."

Chris sniffed and thought about it. "I can only print."

"That'll be fine. Let's sit down."

Abby forced herself not to pace. When Chris climbed into her lap, she had to stop herself from clinging too tightly. With each minute that passed, the empty feeling inside her increased until she knew she was hollow.

She was up and dizzy with fear when the doctor came out.

"A nice clean break," he said to her. Recognizing her anxiety, he gave her shoulder a quick squeeze. "He's going to be a sensation at school with that cast."

"He's... Is there anything else?" Everything from concussion to internal injuries had passed through her mind.

"He's a strong, sturdy boy." His hand still resting lightly on her shoulder, the doctor felt the relief run through her. "He's a little queasy, and he's got some bruises that'll be colorful. I'd like him to rest here for a couple of hours, keep an eye on him, but I don't think you've got anything to worry about. We'll give you a prescription and a list of dos and don'ts. I've already told him he has to stay off wild horses for a while."

"Thank you." She pushed her hands against her eyes for a moment. A broken bone. Bones healed, she thought with relief. "Can I see him now?"

"Right this way."

He looked so small on the white table. She fought back a fresh bout of tears as she went over to hold him. "Oh, Ben, you scared me to death."

"I broke my arm." He was getting used to the idea as he showed off his cast.

"Very impressive." She was already forgiven. Abby could see it in his eyes, feel it in the way his fingers curled into hers. "I guess it hurts, huh?"

"It feels a little better."

Chris walked over to inspect the clean white plaster. "Dylan said I could put my name on it."

"I guess so." Ben looked up for the first time at Dylan. "Maybe you all could. Did Thunder run away?"

"Don't worry about Thunder," Abby told him. "He knows where the grain barrel is."

He stared down at his own fingers, wriggling them tentatively. "I'm sorry."

"No." She cupped a hand under his chin. "I'm sorry. You were standing up for me. Thanks."

He breathed in her familiar scent when she kissed him. He didn't feel so brave now, just tired. "'S okay."

"They want you to stay a little while. I'm going to get your medicine."

"Why don't you and Chris do that, Abby?" Dylan moved closer to the table. "I'd like to talk to Ben awhile."

Because she saw embarrassment rather than anger in Ben's face, she nodded. "All right. We won't be long."

"Can I have a drink?" Ben asked.

"I'll ask the doctor." Bending over, Abby kissed both of his cheeks. "I'm crazy about you, you jerk."

He grinned a little and stared down at his cast. When she glanced over her shoulder from the doorway, he was looking at Dylan.

"I guess you were pretty mad at me," Dylan began.

"I guess."

"Yelling at someone you care about's pretty stupid. Adults can be stupid sometimes."

Ben thought so, too, but he was cautious. "Maybe."

How could he approach the boy? With the truth. He spouted off about honesty, demanded it, expected it. Maybe it was time he gave it. Still cautious, Dylan rested a hip against the table. "I've got a problem, Ben. I was hoping you could help me out with it."

The boy shrugged and began to toy with the edge of the sheet. But he listened.

It was almost dusk when they were home again, settling Ben down and stacking up piles of books and toys for his pleasure. The day had worn him out, and he was asleep before he'd finished his supper. Even while Abby was tucking him in, Dylan carried a dozing Chris up to his room.

"Fell asleep in his pizza," he told Abby with a half grin.

"I'll be right there."

"I can do it. Why don't you do down and fix us both a drink?"

There were a few bottles of wine left over, gifts from Chantel. Abby poured two glasses, then dove into the pizza, realizing she hadn't eaten since early that morning. She was halfway through a piece when the tears started again. She closed the cardboard box carefully, put her head on the counter and wept it all out.

Dylan found her that way and didn't hesitate. He gathered her into his arms, held her close and let her cry against him. "Silly now," she managed. "He's all right. I just keep seeing him in the air, hanging there for that one horrible second."

"I know. But he is all right." He drew her away from him and began wiping away the tears. "In fact, besides one broken bone, he's great."

Abby touched his cheek, then kissed it. "You were great. I don't know what I'd have done without you."

"You'd have done fine." He drew out a cigarette because he was more than a little shaken himself. "That's one of the most intimidating things about you."

"Intimidating?" She hadn't been sure she would ever laugh again, but it was easy. "Me?"

"It isn't easy for a man to get involved with a woman who's totally capable of handling anything that comes along. Running a house, raising children, building a farm. It isn't easy for a man to believe that there are women who can not only do those things but enjoy them.''

"I'm not following you, Dylan."

"I don't guess you would." He crushed out the cigarette, discovering he really didn't want it. "It's all natural for you, isn't it? It's incredible."

She picked up his glass and handed it to him. "If I didn't know better, I'd think you'd already been dipping in the wine."

"I'm just beginning to think clearly."

"I am, too." She picked up her glass and sipped. The wine was unfamiliar and wonderfully cool. "I know you were angry with me this morning."

"Abby—"

"No, wait a minute. The last thing you said to me before Ben came in turned on all sorts of lights. I'd like to get it out now—all of it—and end it."

He could have told her that it didn't matter anymore, not to him. But he could see it mattered to her. "Okay."

"You've asked me why I stayed with Chuck. Very simply, I'd stayed because I'd made a promise. Eventually, when I knew I had to break it and end my marriage, I needed to take all the blame. Somehow it was easier for me to go on believing that I'd made a mistake, I'd failed in some way."

Her voice was strained. Abby took another sip of wine, then continued. "But I hadn't made a mistake, Dylan, and I have two beautiful children to prove it. You said Chuck failed himself and you were right. He was capable of so much more, but he made the wrong choices. It's time I admit that I made the right ones. I've got to thank you for that."

"I'll take your gratitude, but it's not what I'm after."

As it had in the hospital waiting room, her stomach worked itself into knots. "I'll never forget what you did, what you've done just by being here."

"I have a hard time hearing you put all that in the past. Don't you want to know what Ben and I talked about while you were gone?"

She looked down at her wine. "I thought you'd tell me if you wanted me to know." Then she smiled up at him. "Besides, I could always get it out of Ben if you didn't."

"That's one of the things I love about you."

She looked at him with eyes that were clouded and no longer calm. "Dylan, this morning when you were shouting, you said—"

"That I'd fallen in love with you. You have a problem with that?"

She was holding her glass with both hands now, but she didn't look away. "I wish I knew."

"Let me explain it to you the way I explained it to Ben." He set his glass down, then took hers and set it on the counter. "I told him I was in love with his mother. And that I was new at being in love and didn't know quite how to handle it. I told him I knew I'd make some mistakes and that I hoped he'd give me a hand."

He combed a hand through her hair, let it rest on her cheek, then removed it. "I told him I knew a little about running a farm, but I didn't have much experience at being a husband and none at being a father, though I wanted to give it a shot."

Her eyes had grown wide, so wide and vulnerable that he wanted to pull her against him and promise to protect her from everything. But there'd be no rash promises with Abby. She'd had rash promises before, and had them broken. He thought second chances should be based on faith. "Are you going to give me a chance?"

She couldn't swallow. She wasn't even sure how she could still manage to breathe. "What did Ben say?"

Smiling, he reached out and touched her cheek. "He thought it sounded like a pretty good idea."

"So do I." She flung herself into his arms. "Oh, Dylan, so do I."

Perhaps it was gratitude he felt, perhaps it was relief. Mixed with it was a sense of coming home at last. "Just don't start thinking about buying cows."

"No. No cows, I promise." When she laughed, he pressed his mouth to hers. There was everything—love, trust, hope. There were second chances in life, and they'd found theirs.

"Abby..." He could spend hours just holding her.

"Mmm-hmm?"

"Do you think we could talk your father into dancing at our wedding?"

Her eyes laughed at him. "I'd hate to see you try to stop him."

* * * * *

The O'Hurleys—united at last!
Look for THE LAST HONEST WOMAN,
DANCE TO THE PIPER, SKIN DEEP
and WITHOUT A TRACE
coming out this month—
only in Silhouette Special Edition.

FOUR UNIQUE SERIES
FOR EVERY WOMAN YOU ARE...

Silhouette Romance

Love, at its most tender, provocative,
emotional... in stories that will make you laugh and
cry while bringing you the magic of falling in love.

6 titles per month

Silhouette Special Edition

Sophisticated, substantial and packed with
emotion, these powerful novels of life and love will
capture your imagination and steal your heart.

6 titles per month

SILHOUETTE Desire

Open the door to romance and passion. Humorous,
emotional, compelling—yet always a believable
and sensuous story—Silhouette Desire never
fails to deliver on the promise of love.

6 titles per month

Silhouette Intimate Moments

Enter a world of excitement, of romance
heightened by suspense, adventure and the
passions every woman dreams of. Let us
sweep you away.

4 titles per month

From *New York Times* Bestselling author
Penny Jordan, a compelling novel of ruthless passion
that will mesmerize readers everywhere!

Penny Jordan

Silver

Real power, true power came from
Rothwell. And Charles vowed to have it,
the earldom and all that went with it.

Silver vowed to destroy Charles, just as surely and
uncaringly as he had destroyed her father; just as he had
intended to destroy her. She needed him to want her . . .
to desire her . . . until he'd do anything to have her.

But first she needed a tutor: a man who wanted no one.
He would help her bait the trap.

**Played out on a glittering international stage,
Silver's story leads her from the luxurious comfort of
British aristocracy into the depths of adventure,
passion and danger.**

AVAILABLE NOW!

 HARLEQUIN

SIL-1A

Double your reading pleasure this fall with two Award of Excellence titles written by two of your favorite authors.

Available in September

DUNCAN'S BRIDE
by Linda Howard
Silhouette Intimate Moments #349

Mail-order bride Madelyn Patterson was nothing like what Reese Duncan expected—and everything he needed.

Available in October

THE COWBOY'S LADY
by Debbie Macomber
Silhouette Special Edition #626

The Montana cowboy wanted a little lady at his beck and call—the ''lady'' in question saw things differently....

These titles have been selected to receive a special laurel—the Award of Excellence. Look for the distinctive emblem on the cover. It lets you know there's something truly wonderful inside! DUN-1

Silhouette Special Edition

Now appearing
in a special return engagement, Nora Roberts's
bestselling 1988 miniseries featuring

THE O'HURLEYS!
Nora Roberts

Book 1   **THE LAST HONEST WOMAN**   *Abby's Story*
Book 2   **DANCE TO THE PIPER**   *Maddy's Story*
Book 3   **SKIN DEEP**   *Chantel's Story*

And making his debut in a brand-new title, a very special
leading man . . . Trace O'Hurley!

Book 4   **WITHOUT A TRACE**   *Trace's Tale*

In 1988, Nora Roberts introduced THE O'HURLEYS!—a close-knit
family of entertainers whose early travels spanned the country. The
beautiful triplet sisters and their mysterious brother each experience
the triumphant joy and passion only true love can bring, in four books
you will remember long after the last pages are turned.

Don't miss this captivating miniseries—a special collector's edition
available now wherever paperbacks are sold.

OHUR-1A